Playing With My Heart

A SHAKESPEAREAN LOVE STORY

VALERIE WILDING

SCHOLASTIC

For Kate and Richard Harrison
with very much love

Scholastic Children's Books
Euston House, 24 Eversholt Street,
London, NW1 1DB, UK

A division of Scholastic Ltd
London ~ New York ~ Toronto ~ Sydney ~ Auckland
Mexico City ~ New Delhi ~ Hong Kong

Published in the UK by Scholastic Ltd, 2014

ISBN 978 1407 13894 7

Printed and bound in the UK by CPI Group UK (Ltd), CR0 4YY

2 4 6 8 10 9 7 5 3

MONDAY APRIL 5TH 1599

I am so angry, and it is all Miranda's fault. She is the most stupid, loose-tongued friend it is possible to have.

Today is a beautiful spring day, and she stood right by the table where Aunt Sukey was working and asked me to go for a walk along the river with her later this afternoon. I know she just wants to watch the sailors. She is the most dreadful flirt, and will talk to anyone, and Aunt Sukey knows that, too.

So why did Miranda have to say, "Do come – we might find you a sweetheart," in that ridiculous way? I knew she was joking, but Aunt Sukey was kneading bread and didn't see that she was laughing.

"Miranda Coverley!" she stormed. "Get you gone from this house." She picked up the dough and slammed it back on her board. "What Patience's stepfather would say if he heard such nonsense, I do not know."

We soon found out.

As Miranda left, Aunt Sukey called after her, "And only come back when you can behave like a lady!"

Just as she said that, Father came in from the yard to take

a break from work. He kicked his boots off, showering fresh sawdust everywhere.

"Harry Whittingham!" said Aunt Sukey. "Look at my floor!"

He grinned, and she pretended to cuff his ear.

"What's this I hear about behaving like a lady?" Father asked. "You cannot mean my lovely stepdaughters, can you? I can't imagine them ever behaving like ladies."

My sister, Dippity, sitting in the corner, looked up from her stitching. Her face was stricken.

Father laughed. "Don't worry, Dippity, my pet," he said. "You were born a lady. And you have your sweet nature in your favour."

Dear Dippity has little else in her favour. She is not clever. In fact, though she is older than me by two years, she seems much, much younger. But she doesn't know how to be mean or bad. If she ever does anything wrong, it is through ignorance or misunderstanding.

Aunt Sukey pushed her fist into the bread dough. "I was talking to Miranda Coverley," she told Father, adding quietly, "the trollop!" Frown lines creased her pale forehead. Mind, she generally scrapes her black hair back so tightly, I do not know how she manages to frown.

"Is she so bad?" Father asked.

"She is a poor influence on Patience, trying to lead her into bad ways," said Aunt Sukey. "And Patience lets her."

Father looked at me, eyebrows raised. "Then Patience can stay in the house today and help you with the baking," he said.

"The bread's prepared," was my aunt's reply. "She can weed round the blackcurrant bushes instead."

I flounced outside, nearly tripping over Horace, her spiteful grey cat, and began pulling up weeds.

Sometimes I hate Aunt Sukey. Oh, I know she's a good woman, but she is not even my real aunt. Apart from Dippity, I have no blood relations. Our true father was not a hugely rich man, but he and our mother had more than enough money, and a comfortable home. Sadly, our father took to drink and did not work, and the money had all but gone by the time he drank himself to death.

Poor Mother, nearly penniless, married the first good man who asked her. And Harry Whittingham *is* a good man. For when she died of a terrible fever, which I cannot bear to think of, he did not abandon Dippity and me. His aunt came to live with us and care for us, and he has brought us up as if we are his own flesh and blood.

I was just trying to dig out a vicious bramble branch without shredding my fingers, when a quiet voice said, "Let me help you." I turned to see my sister.

I hugged her, being careful not to dirty her bodice. "What would I do without you, dearest Dippity?"

"I don't know, Patience," she said, looking puzzled. "What would you do?"

3

"I just meant—" I smiled at her. "Never mind. You go back indoors. You need clean hands for your sewing, and if you help me you will end up with blood streaks on it."

She nodded and went inside. I wonder if Dippity will ever have a sweetheart and get married. He would have to be a good, kind, understanding man, or he would have me to answer to. She might be slow-witted, but she is gentle and sweet, and would care for her husband.

I worked on, and soon I had an impressive pile of weeds. When I saw Father coming, I fluffed them up so it looked even bigger, then wiped a hand across my forehead as if I was perspiring.

"I'm going back to the yard," said Father. "I have a new apprentice starting tomorrow, so I must make space for him to work." He nodded towards my heap. "You've done well."

"Then may I go down to the river with Miranda later this afternoon?" I begged. "She says those things about sweethearts to tease Aunt Sukey, but she doesn't mean it." This was not strictly true. "We just watch the boats – there is always so much happening down there. One day we saw the Queen's barge go by!"

He looked down at me. "When I've finished in the yard, I have to deliver a small casket to a house near the river. If you can keep Aunt Sukey sweet till then, you shall come with me," he said. "While I spend time with my customer, you can look around for Miranda."

I hugged him, and he went through the gate beyond the flowerbeds to his work yard. Our garden used to be huge but, as Father's work grew, he took over more and more of it for his carpentry yard. So the garden is smaller, but still pleasant, with vegetables, herbs, fruit trees and bushes and, of course, flowers. A rose hedge has been planted so we do not have to look at his hut or his workshop, or the shelter filled with planks of wood, or his cart and barrow and all the other things he keeps there. We can see the horse's stable, where dear old Blossom lives. She has been there as long as I can remember, and she is so old that pulling the cart is all the work she does now. No one rides her, or even rides on the cart any more. But she is sweet-natured.

I got rid of the weeds over the end wall, helped Aunt Sukey clean up after her bread-making, and have sat in the bedroom for nearly an hour, keeping out of her way.

LATER

My walk with Father was a waste of time, because I could not find Miranda. But it was interesting in an unexpected way.

Although Father is a carpenter, and is never short of building work, he is happiest doing what he calls his fancy

5

work. He is artistic and carves wood into the most intricate shapes. On the door of the bedroom I share with Dippity, he has affixed a rosebud and a tiny group of violets, carved from lime wood. The rosebud is for me and the shy violets are for Dippity, because she is shy. They look so real you feel that if you leaned near, you would smell them.

The newest thing Father does is something he learned from a Flemish friend from Antwerp. He gets different-coloured woods and cuts very thin slices, then he shapes these into patterns or even pictures for the tops of tables, or for chests, and exquisite little boxes for ladies. People are surprised at the colours, because not all wood is brown. Ebony is almost black, while boxwood is such a pale yellow, it is almost white at times, and my favourite, pear wood, has a pinkish tinge.

I know he loves doing this far more than building things with great planks and wooden pegs, so I was pleased for him when he said he has been offered work making unusual pieces of furniture and other, rather strange things, like a crown.

"Who would want a crown of wood?" I asked, as we turned right into Thames Street. "It would be very dull."

"Not if it was painted gold," he replied with a grin.

I snorted. That is a habit I am trying to stop, because it is not ladylike, and Father wants me to behave, above all, like a lady. He said it is important for the memory of my mother. "No king would wear a painted crown," I said.

"Not a real king, no," he said, as we turned left into Old Swan Lane, with the river sparkling at the end of it.

I was puzzled. "A pretend king?" I said. And then light dawned in my brain. "Oh!" I cried. "A king in a play! In a playhouse? You are going to do work in a playhouse?"

He grinned. "I am," he said proudly, "and for no less a company of players than the Chamberlain's Men!"

This meant little to me. What matters is that Father is going to work in a playhouse, and that means I might visit there. Oh, how I long to see a play, a real play! All I have seen before was a group of players in the yard of an inn, and I was not allowed to stay because the crowd became rather coarse.

When we reached the home of Father's customer, he told me to find Miranda and to go no further downriver than the steps where the wherries pick up passengers to cross the river to The Bank, in Southwark.

"And no further upriver than Church Lane," he said, "then I'll spot you easily."

Although I didn't find Miranda, I did not mind. The day was warm, and there was much to look at, and I had time to think. How could I persuade Father to let me go to the playhouse? I wondered which one it was. He hadn't said. I know the Theatre in Shoreditch has closed down. But there is the Curtain, and over in Southwark there is the Rose and also the Swan, which I could see from where I stood.

When Father found me, he nodded towards the far side of the river. "That is where my work will be used," he said.

"The Rose?" I asked.

"No, no," he said. "It is a new playhouse, not yet completed."

And that is how I learned that a couple of years ago, the company of players called the Chamberlain's Men had to leave the Shoreditch Theatre when they had problems with the landlord, Mr Allen. It was a bad time for them, and they have had to act in any playhouse they can ever since. But then they discovered that though Mr Allen possessed the land, the actual building was owned by some members of the company. So, in the dead of night, a master carpenter called Peter Street and his men took the Theatre to bits. Each bit was numbered so they would know where it belonged. Every single plank and peg and brick was transported across the river to the south bank. The owner of the land was furious, but there was little he could do about it except curse all the players ever born. Which he did, and Father says he still does.

And now the building is being rebuilt! It will be a brand-new playhouse, and Father says it will be much better than the Rose.

He will not be helping the builders, as Master Street has enough men, but one of the owners of the company, Master Shakespeare, has asked him to do all the fancy woodwork, and to make properties for the players to use when they are on stage. He will make thrones, and crowns, and treasure chests and all sorts of I don't know what. Even swords!

"The thing is, Patience," said Father, "the properties the players use must look real – they must convince the audience. Master Shakespeare said that is my talent, making things look realistic." He smiled. "Remember I made a tiny, ornate casket for him about three years ago – a gift for his wife after his son died? It was for her to keep memories of the boy in – a lock of his hair perhaps, or a baby tooth."

I do not remember. The name is not familiar to me.

"Master Shakespeare was so pleased that he has remembered my skill with wood, and it is he who suggested my name to Richard Burbage and the other members of the company," Father continued. "And who knows, when all the builders have finished and gone, I might still be there, making properties for the stage. And maybe they would employ me to keep the playhouse in good repair. Maybe…"

He would love that, I know. As it is, he must do dull building work for some of the time to make sure he earns enough money to feed and clothe us all. But, as he says, maybe one day he can earn all he needs by doing the work he loves. I am glad I am not a man. I do not know what sort of work I could do. Very little, I am sure, according to Aunt Sukey, who thinks my pastry too hard and my head too soft.

Dippity, of course, can always earn money with her

beautiful sewing and embroidery, and so she does. She is exceedingly clever with her needle, and works so quickly! She can take an ordinary piece of cloth and in a few days or weeks make it look as rich as the Queen's own robes. Not that I have ever seen the Queen, but I have seen the clothes of fine ladies and gentlemen, and they are rich enough. The Queen's must be even richer. All cloth of gold, I imagine, and studded with precious jewels.

Father talked on and on about his dreams, and I must confess I wished he'd stop. All I want to do now is find the right time to ask him about me going to the playhouse. Tomorrow will do nicely.

TUESDAY APRIL 6TH

Hmm. It was a bit too soon to ask Father to take me with him. He is busy with his new apprentice, and had little time for me and my wants.

"You'll have to wait," he said. "A playhouse being built is not a safe place to be."

"But I can't wait."

"Try to live up to your name," he said. "Your sister manages to live up to hers."

Patience! What a name! I have to struggle hard to be patient when I want something. Dippity could never pronounce her real name when she was small, and the name she gave herself stuck. Her true name is Charity, and it suits her. She is good and kind, and never thinks ill of anybody.

WEDNESDAY APRIL 7TH

Miranda called again today. She tapped on the door, looked inside and whispered, "Is your aunt about?"

Then she jumped and her eyes went wide as sizzled eggs when Aunt Sukey, who had been behind the door, looked round and said, "She is, and what of it?"

I ran to Miranda and pulled her in. Aunt Sukey sniffed and went about her work.

"Come and talk to me," I said. "I looked for you by the river the other day, but could not see you. Where were you?"

Miranda ruffled Dippity's cloud of fair hair and sat between us. "My brother and his friends wanted to swim in the river," she said, "so Mother asked me to follow them and make sure they only went where it was safe. They walked a long way upriver, and I was worn out."

"It's safer there, though," I said. "You don't want them swimming near the bridge."

"That's what Mother's afraid of – if they were swept away between the arches we might never see them again. The water rushes so through there."

"You are lucky," I sighed. "Your mother gives you and your brother such freedom."

"I know," Miranda giggled. "It's easy to make her agree to anything we want."

Aunt Sukey walked in at that point with a basket of mending. "If you were my daughter, you wouldn't get round me," she said huffily. "You'll come to a bad end if you're not careful, Miranda."

Dippity put her hand over Miranda's and smiled at her. She looks right into your eyes when she smiles, and you can tell the smile comes from deep inside her – not like some people, whose lips smile, but whose eyes remain cold and hard.

After a moment or two, Miranda looked directly at me with her eyebrows raised. "Shall we walk in the garden?" she asked. "It's warm today."

I guessed she wanted to say something that wasn't for Aunt Sukey's ears, so I jumped up. I looked questioningly at Dippity, but she shook her head. "I need to mend Aunt Sukey's shift," she said.

I know she doesn't mean to, but when she's good like that, it always makes me feel a little guilty. Especially as I was the one who tore the shift when I pulled it off the bushes where it lay drying.

We went outside but, instead of wandering around the garden looking for things to nibble, Miranda edged past Horace, who was lying in wait, watching a bird's nest, then walked straight down to the rose hedge and stood facing it.

"What are you looking at?" I asked. She isn't known for being interested in flowers.

"Ssh," she said. "I want to have another look at your father's new apprentice."

"Why?"

She turned. "Have you not met him?" she asked in surprise.

I shook my head.

She smiled. "I saw him yesterday from my window."

Miranda lives on the opposite corner to us, and her little bedroom window overlooks the yard and the bottom of our garden. What with her one side and nosy Goody Trickett the other, not much is private.

"He is a little older than us," she continued, "and a good deal taller, and *very* pleasant to look upon."

"Well, you will not look upon him today," I said. "He is out with my father."

Miranda's smile vanished and she stamped her foot. "Fie! When will he return?"

I shrugged and asked why she wished to know.

She looked away as if she wasn't really interested.

"I thought you might like to meet him," she said.

Liar. She has seen him and likes his looks. Well, good luck to him. And he need not be vain about it, for she is the same with every young man.

All the same, it has left me curious to look at him.

THURSDAY APRIL 8TH

Aunt Sukey sent me to the apothecary to fetch a package of an unusual herb he had promised her. On the way, I passed Tiny, the little beggar-girl who sits on the corner of our street, in the shelter of the church wall. I call her a beggar-girl, but it's not strictly true, because she never begs. Never asks, anyway, but she does look at people. She has big sorrowful eyes that do all the asking in the world. They are bright blue and are truly striking, with her wispy hair the exact red-brown colour of a squirrel.

"Good day to you, Mistress Patience," she said in her soft, husky voice.

I crouched down to speak with her, dipping my skirt in a puddle of I-know-not-what as I did so. "Good day, Tiny. Are you well?" I asked.

"As well as ever," she said. "How is Mistress Dippity?"

"Busy with her sewing," I said. "Look, she embroidered this handkerchief for me." I took out the piece of fine fabric on which Dippity had stitched two deep pink rosebuds and a full-blown paler pink rose. "Is it not lovely?"

Tiny drew a deep breath, which made her cough a little, and reached for the handkerchief. I let her take it. She held it to her nose and, for a moment, I was afraid she was going to use it as a wipe, but she did not. She simply wanted to sniff the fabric.

"Cor, it is beautiful," she murmured. "I wish I—" She stopped and handed it back to me.

I would have given it to her, but Dippity had only just finished it and Aunt Sukey would have noticed its loss. I resolved there and then to ask Dippity to make some little thing for Tiny, though if I were in the poor little thing's place, I should rather have a good meat pie.

When I had collected the package, which stunk of cat pee (I hope Aunt Sukey intends it for one of her liniments, and doesn't plan to feed it to us) I made my way home.

As soon as I arrived, Aunt Sukey began shrieking at me about the state of my skirt hem. Horace was beside her, hissing at me, and I swear that if he'd been able to shriek, too, he would have done.

Suddenly the garden door opened and in walked Father, followed by a tall young man.

I was grateful for the visitor, because it made Aunt Sukey cease her caterwauling.

Father turned to the young man, swept his arm towards us and announced, "My family!"

Dippity jumped up and bobbed a curtsy.

The young man smiled at her. He has a beautiful smile, and brown eyes that crinkle, just a little, at the corners.

He turned to Aunt Sukey, and greeted her most politely as Father introduced him.

"My new apprentice, Aunt," he explained. "You will see a lot of him. His name is Kit Hamble."

Aunt Sukey's forehead furrowed. "Hamble... Hamble..." she murmured.

Father grinned. "You remember! Kit's father, John, was my oldest friend and, before he died, he asked me to make sure Kit learned to provide for himself. I talked to his mother, Rose, and she told me he loves wood as much as his father did. So I offered to take him as my apprentice. Did I not, Kit?" he asked, clapping him on the back.

"You did, Master," said Kit, "and I am ever grateful. I shall learn building carpentry and, if I may, I shall watch and learn the other wonderful things you do with wood. The beautiful things."

His voice was low and clear and, when he spoke, the very tip of his nose bobbed slightly.

Father introduced Dippity and me, and Kit admired the

work Dippity was doing. "Above all other things my mother loved to sew," he told her, "but her eyesight is not as good as it was. You need good eyesight for sewing."

Dippity looked at him. "Yes, you do," she said. "And you need needles and threads, too."

Kit started to smile, but stopped himself. I think he thought at first that Dippity was making a joke, and then realized that she was serious. I liked him for that. Another man might have been cruel and laughed at her, but he didn't.

Dippity likes him, too. She wouldn't have spoken to him if she did not.

Aunt Sukey invited Kit to stay for some refreshment and, when he left, she wrapped a small cheese tart in a cloth and told him to give it to his mother.

"You are kind, Mistress," he said, then he glanced round at Father, his eyes shining. "I am very fortunate to be apprenticed to such a good man."

"Harry Whittingham is a good man, Kit Hamble," she said. "Do right by him and you will prosper." She pursed her lips. "Do not let him down."

"I never would," Kit said, sounding most sincere.

I did like it when his eyes shone.

TUESDAY APRIL 13TH

I have met Kit Hamble nearly every day, and it is pleasant to have his company occasionally. He is friendly and respectful. The trouble is, I cannot get Miranda Coverley to stay away. Father has a separate entrance to his yard, around the corner, so even when Aunt Sukey refuses to let Miranda in the house, saying we are all busy, she contrives to be lurking about the back gate whenever Kit is there. Clever Miranda, though, always manages to do this when Father is elsewhere.

THURSDAY APRIL 15TH

Kit brought Aunt Sukey a pot of his mother's rosehip jelly this morning. She was so pleased, she immediately fed him a sugar biscuit, hot from the oven. I could tell it was burning his mouth, but he ate it!

I'm glad for Father's sake that Aunt Sukey likes the new apprentice.

MONDAY APRIL 19TH

Today, Father went off to the playhouse with his cart laden
with wood and tools, and he took Dippity with him! Aunt
Sukey says he has had something up his sleeve for a few
days, and it involves my sister. I would have made a terrible
fuss if I had known she was going. As it happened, I was still
abed, fast asleep, when they left. I wonder if he let me sleep
on purpose?

So instead of going to the playhouse – which is not safe
for me, but seems to be safe for my sister – I was sent to Kit's
home with a basket of eggs for his mother. She might as
well move in with us, to save all the to-ing and fro-ing with
various foodstuffs.

Actually, I like Rose Hamble. She is a widow, and frail.
Her home is very simple and plain, and doesn't really look
as if a woman lives there. There are no pretty things like
embroidered cushions or curtains or cloths for the table.
Everything is very plain, which is odd, as any woman can
sew. Even I can embroider reasonably well, though it is not
always a pretty sight!

At first I wondered if she has always been too poor to

afford silks to embroider, but I do not think she is that poor, for Kit is well, if plainly, dressed, and so is she. Then I remembered Kit saying she cannot sew now, as her eyesight is poor, and I felt sorry for her.

Mistress Hamble told me how grateful she is to Father for taking Kit as his apprentice.

"My son is only happy when working with wood," she said. "It is his passion. This is a great opportunity for him to gain some skills that will serve him in good stead all his life. People will always want woodworkers. There is no other material that can do the work wood does."

"Indeed," I said, and she is right.

Then she said how Kit had spoken well of me. I was glad to hear that.

Before I went home, I called on Miranda, and asked what she had been doing. She was, I felt, a little secretive, so I presumed she had been standing around, hoping to see Kit.

"Kit Hamble likes you, Patience."

"He's nice," I said. "I like him, too."

"No, he *likes* you," she said.

I stared at her. "What do you mean?"

"You would like a sweetheart, wouldn't you?" she said, then without waiting for an answer, she went on, "You have one on your own doorstep, should you want him."

What rubbish she does talk. "But *you* like him," I said. "He cannot mistake that."

"I do not!" she lied. "He is too dull for me."

Oh, so he is too dull for Miranda, but he is all right for me. Well, no thank you. I do not want what she casts aside so easily.

When I went indoors, I swept the upper rooms then went to the market for onions, as ours are not ready, and we have none left in store. It wasn't easy to find good ones, as it was late in the day and the sellers were almost sold out. Aunt Sukey said what I got was only fit for pottage. She should have gone herself earlier, that's all I can say. I didn't, of course, speak those words aloud.

Father and Dippity came home with a big basket on the cart. It was full of costumes for the plays that the Chamberlain's Men put on, and Dippity is to make repairs on them! That is what Father has had up his sleeve – some work for Dippity, to keep her occupied and to earn her some money. Some of the costumes belong to the company, and some to individual players. Dippity has been told to take great care of them all, as they are expensive. Father said rich people who enjoy visiting the playhouse sometimes give their cast-off clothes to the players they like best.

"If those are cast-off clothes, I should so like to see their best ones!" I said to Dippity.

She stared. "Rich people have clothes that are finer than these?" She fingered some delicate silvery embroidery on the hem of a doublet. "I should like to see them, Patience."

She often speaks as if I can make anything happen!

Aunt Sukey went next door to take one of our early cabbages to Goody Trickett. She is always giving her little treats, and I believe it is to keep the nosy old crow happy. Goody Trickett watches from her window all day, it seems to me, and will tell anybody your business, especially if she dislikes you. She is always spying on me, asking Aunt Sukey, "Do you allow Patience to do this? Do you permit Patience to do that?"

While they were busy chatting, I went to collect the eggs and found Father fiddling with the henhouse roof. I spoke to him as sweetly and politely as I could.

"Dippity enjoyed her visit to the playhouse," I began. "I asked her what it was like there," I lied, "but all she could talk about was the basket of costumes. Oh dear," I said, gazing into empty air, "how am *I* ever going to find out about the playhouse?"

He was not to be fooled. "You will go there in good time," he said. "Have patience, Patience." He walked off, laughing at his little joke. The same old joke I have heard a thousand times before. I felt like throwing one of the eggs at him.

Then he turned. For a moment I imagined he'd snatched my thought out of the air!

"Instead of gossiping with Miranda all day, why don't you help your sister with her sewing work, Patience?" he said. "I would think favourably of you if you did that."

Oh, I can think of a hundred things I'd rather do. But if it gets me what I want... And I would not have to work *too* hard. Because this seemed such a good idea, I didn't even bother to get angry about him calling me a gossip.

As Father opened the gate into his yard, I caught a glimpse of Kit. He looked very hot as he put down a saw and brushed his hand across his forehead. His hair is the colour of horse chestnuts, and just as glossy. He glanced up and saw me. I smiled at him and he smiled back. His face looked quite pink.

TUESDAY APRIL 20TH

This morning I got up full of new resolutions. I planned to help my sister, but I also had to make sure that Father saw me do it, as I could not rely on Aunt Sukey to tell him something good about me!

After I'd finished my morning chores, I sat down with Dippity. She gave me the hem of a thick skirt to mend. Bless her, she had worked out that this was somewhere my awful stitching wouldn't show!

Straight away, I asked her about her visit to the playhouse, and what was the first thing I found out? That Miranda was loitering outside where they are building. Not only that, Dippity saw her talking to one of the players. He was no one of consequence, just one of the young boys who plays the parts of girls, but I was cross because Miranda has not taken the trouble to come and tell me about it. And I thought we told each other everything.

Actually, I do not tell her everything – I would not be so stupid – but she has always told me everything. She is incapable of keeping a secret. At least, so I've always thought. I shall see if she mentions the boy player when I see her next.

Later, when I was alone, I realized that that was why Miranda is no longer interested in Kit. She has more interesting people to take her attention.

WEDNESDAY APRIL 21ST

I met Miranda down at the fish market. She had no intention of telling me about talking to the boy player. No, that is not fair. I was so eager to find out that I asked her before she had a chance to tell me.

"He was sitting on a heap of stone slabs outside the building," she said. "He was looking at a piece of paper, then gazing upwards and muttering. He glanced my way and smiled."

"Or did you smile first?" I asked.

She laughed. "I do not remember!"

"And?"

"And – nothing."

I grew impatient. "Did you not speak?"

She tossed her head and her hair glinted in the sunlight. Why does everyone but me have shiny hair?

"We spoke," she said, "and he said he admires me." She glanced slyly at me. "He wants me to go there again. He would like to know me better."

I bet he would.

She spun round, nearly dropping her fish basket. "He is so tall and handsome, Patience."

Ha! "He cannot be quite so tall, Miranda," I said. "He was just a boy. Dippity told me."

She rounded on me furiously. "Dippity! What does Dippity know? She would not know a – a fish from a – a flower!"

Now it was my turn to be furious. One thing I cannot bear is people being hateful about Dippity, especially about her not being very bright. It makes my blood rise. And this from Miranda, of all people, who is hardly clever enough to check her change when she is shopping!

"Don't you *ever* speak like that about my sister!" I snapped. And, pulling a fish from my basket, I wiped its wetness across the front of her dress.

"Now go and see if your admirer wants to know you better!" I shrieked.

Then I ran. Miranda can be very vengeful.

MONDAY APRIL 26TH

It is days since I saw Miranda, but I have not missed her, because I have been busy helping Dippity, and talking to Kit. Father is working in someone's house at the moment and has left tasks for Kit to do in the yard. Boring tasks, I think. He just seems to be taking pieces of wood and making them smooth.

"It's important work, Mistress Patience," he said this afternoon when I took him a cool drink. "Wood must be carefully prepared before use. It doesn't matter how fine a carpenter you are; if your wood is not perfected before you start, the work will look rough and poorly done."

"Then it seems a shame that Father gets all the praise for the finished work, when you have done the hard part."

"But that's how I will learn to be as good as he is, Mistress Patience," he said. "That's why I do not mind doing this."

As he spoke, his smoothing tool slipped off the bench. We both bent to pick it up at the same time. Our heads met, and so did our hands.

We both laughed and rubbed our foreheads. Then I said, "You can call me Patience."

He flushed red. And, to my great surprise, I felt my own face grow warm.

Just then Aunt Sukey called, "Patience! Where *is* that girl?"

"Here, Aunt," I called, running back into the garden and up to the open back door.

She gave me a sharp glance. "You look a little hot and bothered," she said. "What could have made you so? Talking? Surely not."

Oh, she makes me so cross. What on earth could she be thinking? I suppose she thinks Kit likes me, too.

I wonder. Does he?

THURSDAY APRIL 29TH

Today I was outside weeding beneath the gooseberry bushes. I hate doing that, as I always end up with my hands in shreds because of the vicious prickles.

I could see through a low gap in the rose hedge that Kit was sitting in the weak sunshine against the hut wall, having his meal break. After a while he came into the garden and offered to help me.

I thanked him, and indeed I was grateful. We worked in silence for a few moments, then Kit commented how nice it was to have the sun on our backs. I was about to reply when I pulled my hand out from beneath a bush, hooking a large prickle as I did so. I cried out when I saw blood on my wrist.

"Let me see," said Kit, taking my hand in his. "There is a thorn still in there."

He gently wiped away the blood with the edge of his sleeve, then pulled out the prickle. It stung a little. He smoothed the back of my wrist with his hand. "There," he said. "All better."

"Thank you," I said. I stayed still. I liked the gentle way he touched me.

He held my hand a moment longer, then we returned to the task.

All afternoon, I kept remembering his gentleness.

FRIDAY APRIL 30TH

I felt odd when I tried to sleep last night. Why did I keep thinking about the gooseberry prickle?

Today, when Kit came in with some apple chutney from his mother, I felt odd again. I wanted to look at him, but I was afraid my face would colour. Then he came across to where I was tying up some lavender bundles for the linen chest.

"How is your wrist today, Patience?" he asked. He took hold of my hand again, just as he did yesterday. I liked it.

I pulled back my cuff and showed him the scratch that was now dark red. "It is almost well, thank you," I said.

Then I glanced up. He wasn't even looking at my hand, but straight into my eyes. I was aware of Aunt Sukey, who had been stirring a cooking pot. Her spoon was still.

Then Kit released my hand, said goodbye and was gone.

I glanced at Aunt Sukey, fully expecting a sharp comment, but she just smiled and turned back to her pot.

You simply cannot guess that woman's thoughts.

WEDNESDAY MAY 5TH

I can just see Kit from our bedroom window if he moves out from the wood shelter. Today is hot, and he is working in just his breeches. His back is turning golden brown from the sun, and he has strong shoulders and arms.

It is almost as if he knows when I am watching, because he will suddenly stop what he is doing, turn and look up. Then he smiles.

Last night, just before I went to sleep, I thought about him. And I fell asleep thinking about his smile.

FRIDAY MAY 7TH

Such a day!

I was up late, and Aunt Sukey had already gone to the butcher's stall. I washed our night shifts, hoping to get in her favour. I was laying them over the currant bushes to dry, and feeling cross because Kit was out working somewhere else with Father, when she returned.

"You have risen, then, Patience," she said sharply.

Oh, I thought, another day of sarcastic remarks, but no! She had something to tell me!

"Your Father left a message," she said. "Dippity must go to the playhouse to collect some more sewing work. She's only been there three or four times, and she's not sure of the way, so you are to take her."

Poor Dippity could hardly miss the playhouse, as you can now see it from this side of the river, and she knows her way to the bridge. But she becomes frightened and confused when she's alone amongst a crowd, and I would not let that happen for anything.

Anyway, this was my chance to go there myself!

I hustled Dippity along, and soon we were ready to leave. I was so excited. I knew I wouldn't be able to see a play, but at least I would see inside, and maybe some players might be practising their parts!

On the way we saw Tiny, sitting in her usual place against the church wall, and greeted her.

"Good day, Mistress Patience," she said. "Good day, Mistress Dippity."

"How is your family?" I asked. She has three sisters and a poorly grandfather and I often forget about them, but being with Dippity always makes me a little bit more thoughtful.

"Well enough, thank you," said Tiny.

Dippity reached into her basket. She took out and unfolded a triangle of soft blue fabric, which she had fringed on two sides, and embroidered with yellow-and-white daisies.

Tiny reached out to touch it. "It's beautiful, Mistress Dippity," she said. "You are so clever, you are."

My sister draped the cloth around Tiny's shoulders.

"I noticed that you cough sometimes," she said. "This is for you. It will help to keep you warm in the chill of the early morning."

Tiny's eyes filled with tears and she reached out her right hand to my sister. Dippity took it and reached down for Tiny's other hand and held both between her own for a moment or two. When she let go and stood up, I saw that one of Tiny's hands was bent, and didn't move quite as a hand should move.

I felt ashamed. In all the years that I have chatted to Tiny as I passed, I have never noticed that one of her hands wasn't right.

As we headed for the river, I said, "Dippity, that was a lovely gift."

"It cost nothing," she said. "The material was left over from a kirtle I made for Goody Trickett, and she bade me keep the scraps. The embroidery thread was my own."

I recalled planning to ask Dippity to make something for Tiny, but couldn't remember actually doing so. I asked her if I did, and she said no.

I have the sweetest sister.

London Bridge was fairly clear, so we walked across it to save paying a penny for a wherry. We would have to take one on the way back if we had a lot to carry.

Aunt Sukey had warned us to talk to no one on the way. "Unsavoury folk live over the other side of the river," she said, though she has, as far as I know, never been there herself. "And other unsavoury folk go there for goodness-knows-what purposes."

I know what purposes. They go to the playhouses, the bear-baiting, the taverns and the gambling houses.

It was easy to find our way to the new playhouse, for it stood high above the surrounding buildings. Not as high as

St Paul's, of course, but as high as the Rose and the Swan. The outside was being painted white, and we approached a pair of tall iron-studded doors with great iron hinges. I wondered if Father had made them, but I thought not, as the studs were not quite regular in their spacing.

"This is the door," said Dippity.

I smiled. "Then let us go in."

Oh, what a sight! It surely cannot be long before the playhouse is ready for plays to be performed.

It is circular, of course, and there are galleries lining the walls almost all the way round. Behind the gallery railings workmen were putting in rows of benches for the audience to sit on. I learned that they will have to pay two pence for this, and if they want a cushion, they may borrow one for a penny more.

There is a vast space in the middle where people can stand to watch the plays. They will be able to do so for just a penny. That seems to me much better value than a seat in a wherry for a trip across the river.

But the thing that really caught my eye was the stage. It juts out into the standing area, and must be at about the height of a man's shoulders, so all would have a good view of the players. Two great columns support the front of a roof that shelters the stage. The ceiling is called the heavens, and is being painted blue, with clouds, stars and a moon.

Behind the stage is the tiring house, where the players

change their costumes and keep the properties – those are the things they use on stage, like a chair, or a shield and sword. The tiring men do all sorts of jobs, like helping the players change costumes between scenes and making sure the props are in the right places. All this I learned today.

Dippity clung to me as I stood and stared. The whole building was alive with activity. Workmen, painters, sweepers, even someone decorating the columns to look like real marble.

Our stepfather was on the stage, talking to a man who looked a little familiar to me. Father was pointing out something to do with one of the doorways that led into the tiring house, and the man listened intently.

Suddenly, Father caught sight of us. He leaned to one side and called to somebody inside the tiring house.

Out came Kit Hamble. Father spoke to him and pointed to us. Kit came to the edge of the stage, leaned down, put one hand on the edge and sprang to the ground.

"Good day, Patience," he said. "And good day, Mistress Dippity. Your father has asked me to take care of you until he's finished talking."

"Who is that man he is with?" I asked.

Kit answered in a hushed voice. "That is Master William Shakespeare," he replied. "He is one of the Chamberlain's Men, and one of the people behind the building of this playhouse."

"He is a player?" I asked.

"Not just a player," Kit said, sounding awed. "He is a poet and a play writer, and many people here say he is the greatest poet England has ever known."

"I think I have met him," I said. "I believe he has been to our house to talk to Father about having something made."

Kit seemed impressed, then his eye was caught by two men arguing off to one side.

"They are players," he said.

"Why do they argue so?" Dippity asked.

He smiled. "They are not really arguing, Mistress Dippity," he said. "They are play-acting. Pretending. They practise their plays in the morning and go off to another playhouse to act in the afternoons. Soon, when this playhouse is ready, they will act their plays here. The first performance will be one of Master Shakespeare's plays, about someone called Julius Caesar, who lived a long time ago."

Father had disappeared into the tiring house, so Kit asked if we would like to see the Lords' rooms.

"Are we allowed?" I asked.

"No one will question us," he said. "Come. This way is safest."

He led me, and I led Dippity, up a stairway to a gallery. Then we walked along a narrow passageway at the back of the benches, into a separate section that overlooked the side of the stage. Dippity clung tightly to me, and I to her, as we were very high up and could easily tumble over the rail.

Then I had a better idea. I clung tightly to Kit!

"Do not fear," he said softly. "I would not let any harm come to you."

The Lords' rooms are to have separate seats, rather than benches, and will have their own door on to the passage, so a servant may be posted there. Kit said the seats will probably cost as much as six pence for each person. You would indeed need to be a lord to spend six pence to sit on a chair for a few hours!

All too soon, Father appeared below, looking for us. We hurried back down to the ground, and he said, "Come, I will show you the costume storeroom."

I followed them up the first flight of stairs to a small, stuffy room crammed with clothes on hooks and rails. Father gave Dippity a small basket of work that had been left by the door for her, then he locked up and showed her a loose board in the floor.

"A spare key is hidden here," he said, "so if ever you need to get in the room when it is locked, you can. Will you remember that, Dippity?"

She nodded and stared hard at the floorboard, as if she was trying to commit it to memory.

"I will remember, Father," I said. "Don't worry about it, Dippity."

She took her basket of damaged embroidery and torn lace down the stairs, and then we had no more reason to stay at the playhouse. I waved goodbye to Kit, and we left.

SUNDAY MAY 16TH

A dreary grey Sunday, with showers every few minutes it seemed. My only outing was to church. Miranda's house was closed and quiet, so the Coverleys must have been visiting relations. Dippity had a headache, so she has stayed in bed. All I had for company today were Aunt Sukey and Father. Not even Kit to brighten the dullness. Oh, such a long, tedious day. And this is supposed to be the merry month of May! I was so bored that I looked through Dippity's basket of work to find something I could do. I spent the next half-hour or so fastening fake pearl buttons on to three pairs of dove-grey gloves. The buttons had come loose and were in danger of falling off, so I have done something useful to help my sister.

Father and Kit spend almost all their working hours at the playhouse now. I love to go there with Dippity. I feel mean saying it, but I am glad she is not sharp-witted enough to go far on her own, because it means I have to look after her. And I truly like to do that, but not just so that I can go to the playhouse with her. I have always been watchful, ever since I was about seven, and began to realize I was more able in my thinking and in my actions than she is.

I do believe Father sets Kit to keep an eye on us when we are there, but I don't mind that at all. I like Kit very much.

TUESDAY MAY 18TH

Today, as Kit and Father arrived back at the yard looking very tired and hot, I took them down a large jug of ale. Kit was giving Blossom a drink, so I handed Father his and he took it to sit in the shade of a plum tree.

As Kit finished with the horse, I went to hand him his ale, but tripped over a loose cobble. As fast as a lightning flash, he reached out and caught me, and half the ale went over him. He did not seem to mind, but held on to me firmly. I looked up at him, expecting him to let me go, but he was looking down at me with those soft brown eyes. We were very close. I stayed still, because I liked being close to him. I tilted my head back, and we stayed like that for a moment. I felt a flutter of excitement, and I wondered, did he feel that, too? Our faces were so close his lips might have touched my nose.

But they did not. He gave the tiniest shake of his head and moved away. I glanced at Father, but he looked perfectly content. He could not have seen us.

I thought that Kit was going to kiss me. I wanted him to. I wanted it very much, because Miranda talks so much of kissing, and I have never done it.

FRIDAY MAY 21ST

Today there was a terrific thunderstorm, with the most torrential downpour of rain. It caught us all out. I was feeding the chickens, and Father and Kit were leisurely making their way up the garden path to the house for something to eat. Aunt Sukey was washing windows and Dippity was putting food out for a stray black cat she likes to feed.

Suddenly, down came the rain. We all rushed for the house. I was last, and when I saw that I was being overtaken by a squawking hen, I gave a scream. I had left the chicken-run open! I ran to round the chickens up, and suddenly found Kit beside me, helping me to catch them. Once we'd got the last one in and shut the little gate, we looked at each other and burst out laughing.

"Drowned rats!" said Kit.

"Don't call me a rat!" I scolded, and pretended to slap him.

He laughed and grabbed my wrist. We fell against each other and I felt his lips brush my forehead. I don't know if it was by accident or design.

"Come along, you two," called Father, and in we went.

That evening, Aunt Sukey made a late supper of bread, cheese and her horrible onion chutney. Father asked what had happened to the apple chutney Rose Hamble had sent. Aunt Sukey pretended she had forgotten it, but I know she had not, for she knew exactly where to lay her hands on it. It was delicious.

As we sat enjoying our supper, Father said, "Patience and young Kit seem to get on well."

I know I went crimson. "He is a good friend," I said.

Aunt Sukey made a funny shape with her mouth, that I have never seen her do before. It gave her dimples.

"Perhaps, in time, he might become more than a friend," she said.

I laughed, but Father smiled. "She could do worse!" he said.

I ripped off a larger chunk of bread than I needed. I hate it when they talk about me as if I am not there.

"Kit is a good apprentice," Father was saying. "He thinks as I do about our work, and what is more, he feels as I do about it."

I was pleased that he thinks so well of Kit.

TUESDAY MAY 25TH

I'm very upset with Miranda. I told her that I am allowed to actually go into the new playhouse, which is true. I also told her that I have been several times, which is also true. Then I told her that I have met all the players and that is not true, but I could not see how she could find out otherwise.

What I forgot is that Miranda always wants what I have, and what I have at the moment is a very good friend. Kit Hamble. And what I did not know (but thanks to Goody Trickett's wagging tongue, I do now) is that Miranda lurks around the corner, in the way she does, waiting to catch him when he goes in and out of the yard. Then, if he is alone, she has the nerve to accompany him on his journey to wherever my father sends him.

I have also learned that if it is the playhouse, she wheedles round Kit, trying to get him to take her inside, which he would not dare to do without Father's permission. I can almost imagine her when he refuses, pouting her lips and swinging her skirts, trying to look irresistible.

And how did I find that out? It began when Miranda leaned out of her window, shrieking at me that I was a liar and I have not met players, and I could not get a sweetheart if I tried because I am such a jobbernowl and a— Well, I would not repeat what else she called me, but I have no wish to speak to her again. Who does she think she is, calling me a liar?

When I told Kit that she has been vile, he said that he would be very glad if she stayed away from him. As he spoke, we moved into Father's hut doorway, as it had begun to spit with rain.

"She makes me nervous," he said. "She asks me questions about you – what you do and where you go – and I am never sure what she is going to do or say next." He hesitated. "She pretended to trip this morning, and I swear she threw herself into my arms on purpose."

I was not surprised. "I hope you did not fall for her trickery and catch her," I said, and I know I sounded a little sharp.

"What did you expect me to do, Patience?" he answered, and I detected a little sharpness in his voice, too. "Should I have let her tumble to the ground?"

I wanted to say yes. Instead, I spun round and stalked away.

"Patience!" he called after me. "Don't run off. Please!"

I stopped. I turned. He was standing in the hut doorway, with his hand held towards me. I glanced up at the sky and walked back, as if I just wanted to get out of the rain. He took my hand and backed through the doorway to make room for me.

I swayed against the wall. He moved closer.

I stretched my face up towards his, but at that moment footsteps rang on the stone path.

"Father!" I said, and stepped away from Kit, who picked up a hammer. We stood there like a pair of confused sheep.

"And what are you two up to?" Father asked jovially.

"I am sheltering from the rain," said I.

"I am polishing this door handle," said Kit.

Father raised his eyebrows. "With a hammer?"

We both blushed, but Father smiled. "Get you gone, Patience," he said. "Kit has work to do."

WEDNESDAY MAY 26TH

It is such a lovely secret I hold, that Kit cares for me. He hasn't said so, but I am sure he must do. I think that, if Father had not appeared yesterday, I would have been kissed.

This evening, when Kit had finished work, I walked part of the way home with him. Knowing that he cares for me, I found it hard to look at him without a big smile on my face.

When he felt I had come far enough, he said, "You must turn back now, Patience."

Instead of turning back, I turned towards him. He leaned down and I swear I felt the warmth of his lips, even though they did not touch mine.

"I must not do this, Patience," he murmured. "I dare not."

"Why?"

"You are the daughter of my master," he replied. "It is not right."

I put my hands on his shoulders. "My father knows that we are good friends," I said. "I know he does. He likes you, Kit. He likes you a lot."

He could not argue with that. Instead, he put a finger to his lips, and then touched it to mine.

THURSDAY MAY 27TH

Miranda called this morning, as sweet as honeyed marchpane, and none of the shrieking of Tuesday.

Until Aunt Sukey went outside, I had to endure Miranda's simpering – and a good number of her sly looks. She had something on her mind, and I wasn't sure I wanted to know what it was. To avoid getting into deep conversation with her, I talked to Dippity about the tiny yellow bows she was making to attach to a lady's bodice.

At last Miranda could bear it no longer.

"I saw you!" she said.

"Saw me what?"

"I saw you kiss Kit Hamble," she said, looking very satisfied with herself.

"You did not," I said, sounding a lot more nonchalant than I felt. "We may have been standing close, but we did not kiss." I felt very self-righteous saying this, because it was true. "Anyway," I said, "what if I had? You have kissed many boys. 'Tis nothing new to you."

I was aware that Dippity's needle was still. I glanced at her. She was looking at me, her eyes wide. Fortunately, Aunt Sukey returned just then, with her arms full of rosemary sprigs and spinach leaves.

Miranda jumped up. "Please let me help you, Mistress Sukey," she said, practically ripping the rosemary from her.

"Thank you, Miranda," Aunt Sukey said, eyeing her carefully. "Is there something you want?"

"Goodness, no," was the reply. "I just came to visit Patience. And dear Dippity, of course."

Father always says your hair will frizz if you tell a lie. I could see Dippity watching for it to happen. I certainly was.

SUNDAY MAY 30TH

Miranda has been in each day, and not even attempted to spy on Kit. She has been up to something, and today, after she'd brought Aunt Sukey a bowl of walnuts which smelled decidedly musty to me, we discovered why.

"I was wondering," Miranda said loudly, "if your father would let me accompany you and Dippity the next time you go to the playhouse. I should *so* like to see inside. What do you think, Mistress Sukey? Would he find any harm in me doing that?"

Aunt Sukey looked slightly bewildered. "I suppose there is no *harm*," she began, but Miranda interrupted.

"Then you will speak to him for me? Oh, Mistress Sukey, thank you so much. You are indeed kind." And she flung me a triumphant glance that said, "*There!*"

I did not care. She might as well accompany us. It made little difference to me.

I have a sweetheart. At least, I think I do. Kit is so busy with Father at the playhouse that I rarely see him during the hours of daylight. But tomorrow, I will go with Dippity to return the basket of costumes she has finished, with my help. I say with my help, but I notice she only gave me work that would not show, and those pieces are at the bottom of the basket.

When Miranda looked at the costumes she said, "Goodness, it is as well I am to go with you. Someone might try to steal these fine things. Especially from such a girl as Dippity," she added in a whisper.

Impudent cat, to speak about my beautiful sister in that way!

"They will not steal from her," I said. "Dippity is very sensible and covers them with an old, ragged cloth."

It was actually my idea to do that, but I will not have anyone speak ill of my sister.

THURSDAY JUNE 3RD

I am all of a dither. Dippity, Miranda and I were at the playhouse. The benches are all finished, so Miranda and I sat on one of the first tier while Master Shakespeare and Master Burbage showed Dippity some drawings for a hanging they want her to make. Dippity is slow with words, but pictures speak to her, so I knew that as long as Father was standing next to her, she would listen to the men and read their pictures. They seemed to be very gentle and kind with her, and when they had finished, Master Shakespeare escorted her back to me.

But before that happened, Miranda stole away while I was talking to the wife of one of the painters. She had brought him a midday meal, and she stopped to sit with me and rub her feet before starting the long walk home again.

When she left, I looked around for Miranda, and there she was, the little cat, talking to Kit in the shadow of one of the doorways that lead to the tiring house. On the stage!

I started towards her, but was brought up short by a voice saying, "Mistress Dippity's sister, I presume?"

I turned, and my heart skipped a beat.

The youth who had spoken has the most beautiful face I have ever seen on any man. His hair is dark and crisply curled, and his eyes the blue of the sky on a hot summer's day, with lashes so long and thick that any girl would cry for them.

I nodded, unable to speak for a moment, all thoughts of Miranda and Kit gone from my mind.

He swept me a bow. "Jeremy de la Motte, at your service, Mistress." Then he looked at me expectantly.

I gathered my wits and bobbed a curtsy, just a little one. If I had curtsied more deeply I fear my legs would have collapsed.

"P-Patience Whittingham, sir," I said. It was only then

that I noticed he was wearing a gown – a woman's gown. He saw me look and glanced down at it. "I have just been measured for length by your sister," he said.

"You are a player, sir?" I asked, realizing he was not much more than eighteen, maybe nineteen, and had no visible growth of beard as yet.

"A player of women's parts," he said, smiling into my eyes. "But I hope it will not be long before I may play men's parts. My voice has become considerably lower than before and already I am finding it difficult to pitch it higher."

I was so flustered I did not think clearly. "You are lovely as a woman," I said.

His merry laugh, his beautiful mouth and even white teeth made me catch my breath.

Fortunately, before I could make a fool of myself, Miranda sauntered towards us and bobbed a curtsy.

"This is my friend, Miranda Coverley," I said. "Miranda, this gentleman is Jeremy…"

"Jeremy de la Motte," he said, sweeping the same bow he had swept for me.

Trust Miranda to interrupt.

Kit and Dippity were standing nearby waiting for me, so all I could do was say farewell to Jeremy and join them. I still felt flustered and hot.

"You speak to the players?" said Kit. His voice sounded a little strained.

"He spoke to me," I said. "Come, Dippity, we must go. Miranda?"

She managed to tear herself away, fluttering her eyelashes so much, Kit must have felt the draught.

He escorted us as far as the bridge. He spoke little, and when our hands brushed, he did not give mine a little squeeze as he usually does.

SATURDAY JUNE 5TH

Father said something that surprised me this evening. I was sitting outside, leaning against the wall by the back door, nibbling some wild strawberries that I'd found behind the pear trees, when I heard Aunt Sukey say that Kit seemed to be turning out to be the best thing that had happened to Father for a long while.

"He is," Father agreed. "And I've been making plans, Aunt Sukey, though I have said nothing to him yet, nor shall I for a long while, probably several years."

"Plans?" she asked. "What plans, Harry?"

I slid closer to the door so I could hear better.

"I would like one day, in a few years," said Father, "to take him as a partner. I think, between us, we can build this into a bigger business, and take on more help. Cut me a piece of that ham, would you?"

I heard the clatter of knife and dish, then Father continued with his mouth full. "I tell you, Aunt Sukey, when the time comes that I can no longer work, it would make me happy to know that the business was to stay in the family. Is there any hope of that, do you think?"

She clattered dishes as she replied, and I could not hear what she said.

It was only when all was quiet that evening, and Dippity was snoring softly, that I thought about this, and realized what Father might have meant.

Does he want me to marry Kit Hamble? Goodness. That thought stopped me sleeping for quite a while. Then Jeremy de la Motte's face floated in front of my closed eyes and I must have slept.

FRIDAY JUNE 11TH

Today, Kit and Father went to a house outside the city wall to measure for some furniture the owner wants in a hurry. It was a lovely sunny morning, and Aunt Sukey was expecting a friend to visit. Dippity was working in our bedroom, because it is easier to spread the hanging out there, so I took a chance and wandered to the playhouse all on my own. It would be no problem for me to be there, as the company and workmen are used to Dippity and me popping in and out. Also, the players are usually busy rehearsing their plays. Today it was the one about Julius Caesar who is killed by his friends in the ancient city of Rome, in Italy.

I had expected a play to be more exciting, with people running on and off the stage, and lots of fights and scenes of love. So far, all I have seen is men making long speeches, waving their arms and sounding very important.

I wanted to see Jeremy de la Motte. I have not stopped thinking about him since the day we met. Is this love? At first sight? I have wondered if I loved Kit, but I never had a moment with him like I had when I first laid eyes on Jeremy.

And there he was, standing in the shade, leaning against a wall. He was wearing men's clothes this time, and again, he saw me before I saw him. My heart leapt at the sight of him smiling at me. He is so elegant. So handsome. And so refined and confident.

When he had greeted me, I was unsure of what to say. "How long have you been a player?" I asked.

"Nearly two years," he said with a grin. "My father thinks I am studying law, so that I can help run our estates."

I must have looked confused (I was), because he went on, "Families like the de la Mottes look down on players.

They do not understand the joy of plays, and of speaking great poetry. When I am a shareholder in the Chamberlain's Men, and when I have played for the Queen, then they might accept it. Until then, I must live this pretence alone." He glanced up. "Ah, I am needed."

Master Shakespeare was beckoning. "Jeremy," he called, "go and read through your part with Thomas."

"At once, Master Shakespeare," Jeremy replied. He bowed, and as he slowly raised his head, his eyes looked deep into mine. Then he was gone. I had to lean on the railing, because my knees felt like a jelly.

The man called Thomas followed, and gave me a sideways glance. I do not like the look of him, even though he appears to be Jeremy's friend. He has a face like a weasel, and I think he would be best playing bad, sly people. Dippity once told me she saw him steal a Banbury cake from a tiring man's dinner box.

Then Master Shakespeare came towards me. I edged back into the shadows, but he was smiling. "We have an urgency, Mistress Patience. Can you write a fair hand?" he asked.

"I can, sir," I said.

I can, too. Our mother was insistent that her daughters be taught reading, and writing as well. Dippity is not at all clever that way, of course, but my writing is clear and elegant, my aunt says. In fact, she says that if my sewing and cooking were as good, I might make someone a decent wife one day.

Master Shakespeare rubbed his hands together. "Will you show me?"

He took me to a little table in the tiring room. It was already supplied with quills and a pot of ink. He gave me a manuscript and asked me to copy it out on the back of a used piece of paper.

I examined the manuscript. "The writing is untidy," I said, "but I can read it."

He looked amused. "I am glad it is not too bad," he said, "as the writing is my own."

I should have been embarrassed, but he smiled and pushed the ink pot towards me. As I picked up the quill and began to copy, I was conscious of someone else behind me.

After I had written a few lines, Master Shakespeare leaned over to examine my work. "That looks good enough to me," he said, then he spoke to the person behind. "What think you, John?"

A man moved into view. He had one arm tucked inside his jerkin, and looked most uncomfortable. He took the paper from me. "It is reasonably clear," he said, and walked away.

Master Shakespeare explained that the man called John is the company's scrivener. It is his job to copy out all the words for the players, but he has hurt his shoulder badly, and is in too much pain to write at the moment.

"If you would like to ask your father," Master Shakespeare

went on, "there is employment here, copying out parts for our plays. John would oversee the work."

My heart jumped at the thought of being able to spend time in the playhouse officially! "I need not ask my father, sir," I said. "He would be happy for me to do the work."

"For which you will be paid," said Master Shakespeare, "but I cannot agree to you being here with all these rascals –" He waved a hand at a bunch of players practising a sword fight with wooden sticks "– without your good father's permission. I have too much respect for him."

"Then I will go, sir," I said, "and find him, and ask him."

Master Shakespeare looked around. "Where is your friend with the red-gold hair?"

"Miranda, sir? She is at home, I imagine."

He smiled. "It is best that you come with your father or sister to do your work, rather than your friend. It will be less distracting for you. Good day, Mistress Patience." He turned to go, then looked back. "Miranda? It is an unusual name."

I told him what she had told me. "Her mother's name is Mirabel and her father was Andrew. They blended the two names together."

"Ah," he said. "I see. Miranda." He repeated her name, slowly, as if he were rolling it around inside his mouth.

And he was gone.

So was I – like the wind. I flew home and waited impatiently for Father, so I could tell him about my meeting with Master William Shakespeare. As I waited, it suddenly struck me that I am (I hope) going to do work for the most famous play writer and poet in London!

When Father came home, he listened and did not seem displeased at the idea. He said he will give me his reply tomorrow.

Red-gold hair, indeed. Golden it might be, but those red strands are more like orange.

MONDAY JUNE 14TH

When I go to bed at night, my thoughts are full of Jeremy de la Motte. I love his name. I play with it in my mind. De la Motte. Jeremy de la Motte. Patience de la Motte. Oh, goodness!

Father is allowing me to work for Master Shakespeare. I think he admires him so much that he would agree to anything Master Shakespeare wanted.

John, the scrivener, is in much pain, poor man, and I think it makes him crotchety. He sits near me as I work, and I try my hardest not to make any mistakes, and to write in my best hand. I also try my hardest not to get annoyed when he is pickitty about my writing.

I have to write out all the sections of words a player says, but I must also, before each bit, write out the words another player speaks before him. This is called the cue and is very important because it tells the player when to say his piece.

Jeremy de la Motte called in this afternoon to ask if his part was ready. I waited for him to come to speak to me, but the scrivener sent him away with a flea in his ear, saying, "The important parts will be ready first, boy. Go and oil your corsets." This made me laugh to myself. Jeremy glowered at the man, though he did not let him see the glower. And though I could see his teeth were clenched, maybe in anger, he winked his eye at me.

Oh, those sparkling eyes. My stomach squirls as I think of them.

TUESDAY JUNE 22ND

Today Miranda called from her window as I stood outside our gate. I was waiting for Father and Kit to appear, as we were all to go to the playhouse together, so I went to speak with her. I have inky fingers, and she noticed this.

"Patience! Where are you going with hands in that state?" she asked.

"I am going to the playhouse," I said.

"Then I shall come."

"I think not," I said. "I am going there to work, and cannot have a friend to accompany me."

"Work? What are you talking about?"

I heard the cart coming out of the yard, so I left her with a cheery, "Farewell, Miranda," and joined Father and Kit, walking alongside Blossom.

Kit said little on the way, and Father clearly noticed, for he asked him, "Are you well?"

"Well enough, I thank you, sir," was the reply.

I touched Kit's arm, and was rewarded with a warm glance.

"Are you still my friend?" he asked, in a low voice so Father could not hear.

"Of course I am," I replied.

I felt my face flush. I did not know what to say to fill the silence. My feelings are confused. I am fond of Kit, but I cannot chase Jeremy from my thoughts.

He was not at the playhouse. Few of the players were expected until late morning, when they were to discuss who was taking which part for a play. They must learn several plays, because when the playhouse is open, they will perform a different one each day. I could never learn so much. It's very easy for boys to learn things by heart; they do so much of it at school. But me, I can hardly remember what I have to get in the market.

I worked hard for half of the day, then set out alone for home carrying a torn fur-trimmed robe for Dippity to mend. They have sewing people in the tiring house, but Dippity is entrusted with the finest of the costumes. She showed me her hanging. It is to be suspended across the central entrance on to the stage, and will represent a forest. There will be a roe deer embroidered on it. Such skill, and she is only eighteen. How can people be so cruel as to laugh at her because her wits are slower than theirs?

Dippity has never had much learning, but I have learned much from her. Apart from the fact that it really is possible to be good and kind to everyone (something I can never manage, however) I have learned that everyone can be clever at something. It is just a matter of luck whether or not that thing is discovered. I wonder what I am clever at.

THURSDAY JUNE 24TH

Dippity came with me to the playhouse today. Father and Kit stayed in the yard, working on playhouse properties. I have seen a fine Venetian gondola being made. It will fool the eyes of all who watch the play, but if you looked closely you would see many holes, so it would surely sink.

I think the playhouse building must be almost finished. There are fewer workmen than ever before, and the fine weather has been helping plaster and paint to dry quickly. Today, players lolled around on the benches or lay on the stage, practising their words – many of which I had written out myself. Nobody seemed to have difficulty reading my handwriting.

When I stopped for a break, I sat in a sheltered corner in one of the Lords' rooms to eat my bread and cheese. No one could see me, or so I thought. After a few minutes, I heard a low whistle, so I looked across at the window of the hut above the stage roof. There is to be a cannon there one day, and there will be all sorts of contraptions for making special sounds, like thunder.

Whose face should be poking over the window railing, but Jeremy de la Motte's! He winked at me, making my stomach squirl again, and beckoned to me.

I shook my head. I had no idea how to get to the hut, otherwise I think I might have gone. He disappeared from view, and I sank out of sight behind the railing of the Lords' room, finished my cheese, and was just biting into my apple, when two hands covered my eyes.

I laughed. "Jeremy!" I cried, pulling his hands away and turning to look up at him.

But the eyes I looked into belonged to Kit.

It wrenched my heart to see that I had hurt him terribly. That much was clear to me.

"Kit!" I begged, as he went to leave. "I only said it was Jeremy because his was the last face I saw, looking at me. I did not know you were here, or I would have known it was you." None of that was true. I knew that I had said "Jeremy" because his was the face I most wanted to see.

I feel for Kit, but the thing is – Jeremy is so exciting. He makes my heart beat faster. With Kit I just feel... I don't know. Comfortable.

When he left me, I heard his feet pounding on the staircase, then I saw him run across the yard in front of the stage and out of the big double doors. No sooner was he out of sight, than Jeremy was beside me.

"You are sad," he said and, joining me down on the rough wood floor, he pulled me to him. I nestled against his silk-clad chest and wondered if he could feel the pounding in my breast.

He put a finger beneath my chin, tilting it up towards him. I sensed he was going to kiss me. Oh, I wanted his kiss so much!

He wanted it too. He lowered his face to mine, and our lips met. At first, he was soft and gentle, and I felt as if I might faint. But then his mouth moved over mine, pressing harder, and I could feel the tip of his tongue exploring the place where my lips met.

He pressed me to him, groaning a little, and then his tongue pushed between my lips. I did not know how to respond to such passion. I had never been kissed before, and this was not as Miranda had described it, and definitely not the tender moment I had expected. I felt uneasy and pulled my head away.

To my relief, he did not question me. He just looked deep into my eyes and said, "You are beautiful, Patience."

"Pardon me," said a voice. I looked past Jeremy's ear to see my sister looking down at us.

"Dippity!" I said. "How did you know where I was?"

"Kit told me you were here," she said. "He said he was coming up to see you. Are you all right, Patience? What are you doing on the floor? Can you not stand? Do you feel ill?"

Quickly, Jeremy said, "Your sister felt faint, so I lowered her down, but I believe she is better now." He helped me to my feet.

"I am well," I said. "Come, Dippity, we must go."

"Wait," said Jeremy. "I will walk with you to the river, and you must have a wherry to take you across."

I thought that was very kind of him.

When we reached the landing stage, Jeremy discovered he had no money on him, so I was forced to pay the boatman. No matter. I have money now, from my writing work.

On the way, I made Dippity understand that she was not to mention Jeremy de la Motte's name at home, especially when Kit was around.

"I understand," she said.

Unfortunately, she understood too well. When Father

asked how her work was going, she told him what she had done that day. Next, he asked me, and I explained what I had learned, and how well my writing had gone.

Then Dippity said, "Patience felt faint."

Aunt Sukey looked up anxiously. "Oh? You did not tell us, Patience."

"I did not worry," said Dippity. "She was well looked after."

"Who by?" asked Aunt Sukey, as I frantically tried to kick my sister under the table.

"By somebody," said Dippity.

Father frowned. "Who is this somebody?"

"I cannot say his name."

"Dippity," said Father, eyeing me, "we need to know how Patience was looked after."

I was groaning inside.

"Somebody lowered her to the floor, and then somebody got down on the floor beside her and—"

"Enough!" said Father. "Patience, upstairs. I will speak with you later. Dippity? To your mending."

When Father came to the bedroom, he looked at me and said, "It's the de la Motte boy, isn't it?"

"He's not a boy," I said. "He's a young man."

Father's face was furious. He is good and kind, but he expects us to respect him, and insolence is something he will not tolerate.

"You will stay in the house for a week," he said. "You

63

are to go no further than the garden gate, except to church on Sunday."

"But what about my work?" I asked. "I must not let the company down!"

"If Master Shakespeare can trust you with his manuscript, I will bring it here," he said. "You can write just as well in your bedroom. And while you are here, think about what you are doing to Kit."

I burst into tears. I couldn't think of anything else to do.

But when I was alone, I had time to think about the day, and I hugged my secret to myself. I have been kissed!

SATURDAY JUNE 26TH

It is my second day cooped up in the house like an old hen. I have laundered, I have cooked, I have weeded, I have gathered, I have swept. This afternoon I slipped upstairs to rest for a while, but no sooner had I sat on the bed than Aunt Sukey called from below.

"Patience?"

I make it a rule to wait until she calls me a second time because, just occasionally, she gives up after the first shout. Not this time.

"Patience!"

I moved to the doorway. "Yes, Aunt?"

"You have a visitor."

Tired of the house as I am, I was not keen to see Miranda. She would gloat about her freedom, and say, "Kit this," and "Kit that," in an effort to make me jealous. I am a little jealous, because he is supposed to be my friend, but she is welcome to flirt with him all she likes. My feelings are elsewhere.

I walked downstairs – rather, I slummocked down, as Aunt Sukey put it – only to find that my visitor was not Miranda at all. It was none other than Master Shakespeare!

"Good day, Mistress Patience," he said, with a smile.

I curtsied. "Good day, Master Shakespeare."

"I understand from your father that you are, er, indisposed," he said, "yet you are well enough to continue your work."

I blushed, I know, because I was hoping he did not know the reason for me being virtually imprisoned in my own home.

He turned to Aunt Sukey. "May I make use of your table, madam?" he asked.

She smiled. "It would be an honour to have it used by the greatest play writer in London."

He made a waving-away gesture at the compliment, but made no attempt to deny it. Instead he laid out a manuscript and a pile of paper, and asked if I would write the parts as quickly as possible.

"See?" he said. "Here's the list of characters in the play. There is enough paper here for each of them. You understand about cues? Good. Do you think you can do that? Can your aunt spare you for the amount of time it will take?"

Aunt Sukey was so impressed at meeting an important member of the Chamberlain's Men that she would have said yes to anything. And I would rather read or write than wash vegetables, which was to be my next task.

Master Shakespeare added ink and quills to the pile on the table then said, "Perhaps you would walk me to the gate, Mistress Patience?"

As we went along the path, he asked, "Where is the young man I have seen you with?"

"Jeremy?" I said, thinking that Master Shakespeare should know that better than me. "I expect he is at the playhouse."

"No, not de la Motte," he said. "I mean your father's apprentice."

"Oh," I said. "Kit. He is working at a house in Tower Street today."

We had reached the gate.

"He is a fine young man," said Master Shakespeare. "I understand that Kit has a good future, and that it is likely that he will exceed even your father's reputation and skill."

"I suppose so."

Master Shakespeare paused with his hand on the gate, and gazed up at the sky. "Jeremy de la Motte, now," he said. "He will be a fine player – he is already good – but…"

I waited.

"Patience, remember – all that glisters is not gold," he said. "Good day to you."

Whatever was he talking about?

TUESDAY JUNE 29TH

Today, I was working on Master Shakespeare's play when Miranda called.

"I saw your aunt and sister leave the house," she said brightly, as she bounced up to me. "Whatever are you doing?"

She leaned over my work. "Odsbodkins! That looks dreary. Leave it and come out for a while. There are ships unloading on the river, the sun is shining and we can—"

"Thank you, Miranda," I said, "but this work is too important to be left. Master Shakespeare requires it for rehearsals as soon as possible."

I did enjoy the expression on her face. And I am glad

I had an excuse not to go out, so I did not have to tell her I have been ordered to stay inside. But when I went to the window and breathed the air, I thought how nice it would be to go for a walk.

If I finish the manuscript work without fuss, I am sure Father will let me take it to the playhouse. I will tell him I need to, because Master Shakespeare sometimes wants changes, so I must be there to do them. I am sure that Master Shakespeare could easily make his own changes, but Father does not know that.

LATER

All finished! And Father *will* let me take it to the playhouse myself! I am to escape at last!

WEDNESDAY JUNE 30TH

"You are to avoid that young player, Master de la Motte," Father said before I left this morning. "Many players have bad reputations and—" He held up a hand to stop me saying anything. "Yes, I know that William Shakespeare has a good reputation, but I am quite sure that even he is not a saint, especially with his wife and family far away in Stratford. The point is, Patience, that if you become known as a girl who keeps company with players, your own reputation will be soiled."

"I understand, Father," I said. It was the best thing to say in the circumstances, or he would not let me go, and my heart was leaping at the thought of seeing Jeremy again. I have never known anyone like him. He is – exciting.

"One more thing," said Father. "Dippity is to stay with you at all times. Do you understand that, Dippity?"

She nodded. "Yes, Father. I will stay with Patience at all times."

I went upstairs to fetch my basket. I had carefully placed each completed sheet of paper in it as soon as the ink had dried thoroughly. I laid a cloth over it – it would never do to have it splashed by water, or something worse being thrown from a window. As I came downstairs, Father said, "One more thing…"

I had to stop myself rolling my eyes. How many one-more-things?

"Yes, Father?"

"Miranda is not to go into the playhouse with you. I know you cannot stop her walking with you, but that is as far as it goes."

"Yes, Father."

Dippity and I left the house. I waved to Kit, who was just rounding the corner, taking the cart laden with long, straight logs to the yard. He stopped Blossom for a moment, then turned away and carried on. He probably thought I might go and talk to him, but I did not have time.

Within two minutes, I sensed someone close behind me. Next moment, I felt a tap on my shoulder. I spun round.

"Miranda!"

She laughed and slipped between me and Dippity. "Where are you going, Patience?" She flicked the cloth aside and peeped into my basket. "Oh, writing things, how dull," she said.

Dull! She should read some of Master Shakespeare's words. Though I cannot always follow his meaning, I have learned many new words through copying his work. And when I hear snatches of his writing spoken by the players, it comes alive, and suddenly I understand it.

But, as I know Miranda cannot read, I said nothing of this, but simply asked where she was off to.

She shrugged. "Nowhere." Then she took my hand. "I shall come with you! You are taking your sister to the playhouse, are you not?"

I did not like to say that Father had forbidden me to take Miranda, so I said, very clearly for Dippity's benefit. "I am not allowed to take you, but if you wish to follow me, I cannot stop you." I reached across her and squeezed Dippity's hand. She smiled happily.

Secretly, I was pleased Miranda was coming, because she would see that I am valued by the Chamberlain's Men, and she would see how much Jeremy likes me. She, who is always looking for a sweetheart, would see that one came to me unbidden.

She asked about Kit.

"I have scarcely seen him," I said.

"Except for this morning," said Dippity.

Miranda eyed me as if to say, "Were you lying to me?"

"Dippity is being truthful," I said. "I did *see* him this morning, but that is all."

"Do you not care for him any more?" Miranda asked.

I shrugged. I could not say no, for I am indeed fond of him, but it is Jeremy who has stolen my heart.

We entered the playhouse, which is to be called the Globe. How different it looked today. Most of the building work is done, and the thatchers are hard at work finishing the roof. The stage reminds me of a great bird coming towards me. The broad entrance at the back is flanked by two smaller entrances, like wings. Curtains are draped over the arched wing entrances, but the main entrance is covered at the moment by Dippity's beautifully embroidered hanging of the roe deer in the forest. My heart swelled with pride when I saw it. Dippity herself stood entranced.

"Look, Patience," she breathed. "It is my work. The Chamberlain's Men have put my work on their stage. Everyone can see it."

"It's pretty," said Miranda, but her eyes were all about, watching the players having an argument about who should stand where. Another player, in a long coat, did a funny dance around them, making faces, but they ignored him. I think they have seen all his jigs before.

I gave my sister a hug. "Dippity," I said, looking directly into her eyes so I could be sure she understood, "hundreds – no thousands of people will visit this playhouse and they will all see your work."

"They will?" she said, eyes wide and shining.

"They will. People will come from all over London to see the plays, and your hanging will be right there, every day."

A voice beside me said, "It won't be there every day…"

I turned. It was Master Shakespeare.

"Oh," I said. "I thought—"

He grinned. "We must exchange it for another, each time we change the play. And for that reason…" He turned to my sister. "…we would like Mistress Dippity to create another hanging for us," he said. "This time it will be a simpler one. A plain black background, upon which will be an eagle with outspread wings."

Dippity could not speak. I could see that she was thrilled. Then her face fell.

"What is it?" I asked.

"I do not know what an eagle looks like," she whispered.

Master Shakespeare took her hand. "One of the company will draw it. All you need do is copy it and bring it to life."

Her face brightened.

He turned to me, and indicated my basket. "You have brought the players' parts, Patience?"

I lifted the cloth. "Indeed, sir."

"Then perhaps you would be kind enough to take them into the tiring house and give them to John, the scrivener. Maybe it will bring a smile to his sour face!"

He smiled and wandered over to the group of squabbling players.

I glanced at Miranda. She seemed awestruck.

"You truly are working for the company?"

"Did I not tell you?" I said airily. "Dippity, you must go and see if there is any other needlework for you."

She went off by herself into the tiring house. She is becoming so confident.

"Wait here, Miranda," I said, "while I deliver my work. You can watch the players rehearse."

There was no need to tell her that. She was gaping at them already.

I followed Dippity into the tiring house, and a minute later I ran back out, with the scrivener's angry voice shrieking after me.

I had brought the players' parts, but I had forgotten Master Shakespeare's precious manuscript. The only fair copy of the whole play! He had entrusted it to me, and I had left it in my bedroom. Why, at that very moment, Aunt Sukey might be using it to wrap her new cheese in!

I yelled at Miranda, "I will be back anon! Look after Dippity! Do not let her out of your sight! Do NOT!"

I was dimly aware that the players had stopped and were staring at me. Miranda nodded, tossed her hair, and leaned back against the barrier that separates the benches from the standing area. I swear she was deliberately thrusting out her bosom. I saw that weasel-faced Thomas making his way over to her.

I ran from the playhouse, but soon slowed to a brisk walk. I should be worn out if I ran all the way, and Dippity was quite safe.

Before I reached the bridge, I heard my name called, and if my heart could sing, it would have burst into a joyful air right then and there.

Jeremy! He hurried through the crowd towards me, took my hand and kissed it. His lips lingered, and I so wanted them to be on mine.

"I will walk with you," he said.

I felt a little guilty, but there was small chance of meeting Father, so I put my guilt in a little imaginary box and threw it over my shoulder.

Jeremy's arm encircled my waist and, as we walked, I turned to gaze into his sparkling eyes. They glittered darkly, and a tremor ran through me. I wanted to lean into him, but dared not.

We spoke little, just walked together. Suddenly, he swerved into the entrance to an inn yard. It was cool and quiet there. He swung me round until I was against the wall with his body close to mine. He put his hands against the wall just above my shoulders, so I would have had to duck under them to escape him.

I had no desire to escape. His breath was warm on my skin as he lowered his face to mine and kissed me, hard and long.

I felt his tongue move from side to side and, gradually, my lips parted, just a little. He pressed his body closer to mine and I wondered if he could feel the beating of my heart. Did he know how my legs trembled?

His hands caressed my back, then, as he whispered into my ear, telling me I was the loveliest little thing he'd ever seen, one hand moved lower, to my waist, then lower still. He pressed me to him, and I felt so weak-kneed, I thought I would fall to the ground if he let me go.

As Jeremy's teeth nibbled at my ear, I looked over his shoulder and saw an old woman staring at us. She caught my eye and smiled. Was she remembering her first love? Was she envying me? I felt proud to be loved by such a handsome young man.

Jeremy's lips sought mine again and his hands slipped round to grip my waist. As they slowly moved up my sides, he moaned softly and I caught my breath.

"Stay still," he murmured. "The world will wait."

I suddenly came to my senses and gasped. "Master Shakespeare! He is waiting for his manuscript!"

I pushed Jeremy away. He stood against the wall for a moment and watched my hands as I straightened my bodice, then said, "I will accompany you."

"Just part of the way," I said. "If my father saw us..."

He never heard what would happen if my father saw us, because his lips were seeking mine again.

As we drew nearer to my home, arms round each other's waists, I became nervous, in case Father or Aunt Sukey should suddenly appear. But Jeremy is so thoughtful. He sensed that I was uneasy and said, "I shall go back. It is time I was elsewhere, anyway."

We parted. He went down the street and I walked towards home. At the gate I turned and looked back to catch one more glimpse of that handsome figure, but instead, had a shock. Kit was right behind me. He almost bumped into me! He grasped my waist to prevent me falling. But he did not let go. His hands remained where they were and he looked down at me. I do believe he might have been thinking to kiss me. I peeled his hands from my side. I did not want them where Jeremy's hands had so recently rested.

"How are you, Patience?" he asked.

"I am well, I thank you," I replied.

"And Dippity? She is well?"

"She is at the playhouse."

Kit paused. "At the playhouse? Alone? Your sister will be nervous and frightened on her own," he said. "She will be afraid she might get lost. I will go and fetch her. This is my meal break."

Honestly, I wished he would not interfere. Dippity was perfectly safe because Miranda was with her. But if I told him that, Kit might tell Father, and I had been forbidden to let her into the playhouse with us.

"You need not go," I said, "because I am going straight back there as soon as I have collected something from my bedroom for Master Shakespeare."

I thought he might have asked what I had for Master Shakespeare, but he seemed only concerned about Dippity.

"Then be quick," he said, but he sounded calmer now.

I collected the manuscript and hurried back to the river, but as I was crossing the bridge, who should I meet but Miranda.

Alone.

"Where is Dippity?" I cried. "Have you lost her? Say you haven't!"

My heart began to thump. Before Miranda had a chance to answer, I was already picturing my darling sister lying wounded in some stinking alley, or ... oh, it did not bear thinking about.

"Where is she?" I screamed, my fingers digging into Miranda's arm.

She yanked herself free. "I don't *know* where she is," she snapped back. "All I know is that when I went to look for her, she wasn't there. I looked behind the stage, and I looked along all the benches. The players are gone and it is all quiet except for the men painting the outside."

"She *must* be there!" I cried over my shoulder as I raced towards Southwark. "Dippity isn't brave enough to go off on her own."

"It's not my fault!" Miranda cried, running after me. "That horrible Thomas kept me talking, and then I lost my pouch with my money in. I'd only put it down for a minute, one of the workmen must have taken it, and I was looking for it and then I realized she was gone..."

"She *must* be there!" I shrieked. "She would never have left the building on her own."

Miranda had spoken the truth. The playhouse was quiet. I raced into the tiring house, but there was no sign of her.

"The hut!" I cried, remembering the little room above the stage roof. I flung the manuscript on the scrivener's table and hurtled up the stairs, Miranda close behind, still wittering on about it not being her fault. I threw open the door to the hut.

It was empty.

"Maybe she's hiding in the Lords' rooms," I said.

"Why would she hide?" Miranda whined.

"She'll be too frightened to move," I snapped, heading back downstairs.

Just as I reached the landing, I heard a noise coming from the costume storeroom. I tried to open the door, but it was locked.

For a moment I considered trying to break the lock, thinking Father could easily mend it. But thinking of Father reminded me – the loose floorboard! I looked around, found it and, to my intense relief, the key lay beneath.

In moments I had my beloved Dippity in my arms. The poor thing had huddled up in the far corner with her face buried in her hands.

"Locked in," she cried. "Scared! Scared!"

"You're safe now, darling," I whispered to her. I don't know who was shaking most, but when Miranda whined again, "It wasn't my fault!" I felt like punching her.

By the time we reached home, with moaning Miranda trailing behind, I had talked very carefully indeed to Dippity. I had told her she must forget what happened, and then she would feel better. "Say nothing about it to anyone," I said.

Somehow I knew that if it came out, I would get the blame.

What I said to Miranda is best not written down, but I don't think she will be telling anyone.

Sharp-eyed Aunt Sukey looked at Dippity's pale face as soon as we went indoors and said, "Whatever is wrong?"

I am amazed at how quickly I gathered my wits. "She is upset because we left the sewing work at the playhouse."

"No, Patience," said Dippity. "There was no work for me. I went up to the storeroom to look and there was no basket."

Her eyes filled with tears.

"There, there, don't be upset," said Aunt Sukey. "There will be work another day. Go and see if there are any cherries ripe yet. You know how you love to hang them on your ears, like jewels."

Whew!

FRIDAY JULY 2ND

I met Kit as I left the fish stall on the riverbank today, and he asked if Dippity had been all right when I returned to the playhouse.

"She was perfectly well," I said, trusting that God would forgive the lie, "but I thank you for your concern."

He was quiet for a moment, and seemed to be searching

for something to say. Instead, he reached out a hand and tried to take mine in his. I confess I would have quite liked him to hold my hand – he is so gentle – but it seemed disloyal to Jeremy to do so. Anyway, suppose Jeremy had seen me? So I pulled back.

Suddenly, Kit's eyes turned away from mine and glanced over my shoulder.

He scowled slightly. "Oh, no," he muttered, and without warning, he was gone!

I was convinced he had seen Jeremy and looked round in expectation, but I only saw, in the distance, Miranda, with her mother's market basket.

"Patience!" she cried, when she reached me, as sweet as honey. "Were you not just talking to Kit? I swear you were."

I nodded.

"Then where is he? He has gone!"

"He came to give me a message from Father," I lied, "and he had to hurry back."

Miranda looked quite disgruntled, which gave me a lot of pleasure.

WEDNESDAY JULY 7TH

Father sent me to take a crown and a shield to the tiring house today, and said he would be along later. He has to finish carving a casket for a French princess in a new play that Master Shakespeare is writing, called *Henry the Fifth*.

Some of the players were trying on costumes for this play, and I was turned away from the tiring-house door once I had passed in the properties Father had sent.

I wandered out of the playhouse and thought to take a look at the bearpit, where I have never been. Aunt Sukey says such spectacles are not for the eyes of young girls.

I had walked no more than a few paces when who should bounce up to me but Miranda, looking as pleased with herself as a small child with a dish of sweetmeats.

She had not one, but three, young men in tow. All seemed unable to take their eyes off her. One, the plainest, turned his attention to me, and Miranda started flashing her eyes back and forth as if to say, "Go on, this is your chance, Patience."

But I had no eyes for those soft boys. For along came my Jeremy, walking with a swagger and a wicked twinkle in his eye.

He swooped upon me, circled his arm round my waist and swept me into his arms. Then, right in front of Miranda, he planted a firm kiss upon my lips.

He let me go, bowed and said, "I must leave and attend the playhouse now. Goodbye, fair Patience. Until we meet again … I must have … patience."

I stood for a moment, gasping with the delight of it all. Not just the kiss, but the sight of Miranda, gaping at me with her mouth most unattractively open.

I set off towards the bearpit, walking at a fair speed, and heard her running up behind me.

"Patience, you are … you are…"

"I think I shall buy something to eat," I said, eyeing the stalls around the pit. "I feel very hungry all of a sudden, and I think I should like a mutton pasty. Something seems to have given me an enormous appetite."

"You and Jeremy de la Motte?" she said. "You are in love!"

I swung round and gripped both her hands, hard. "Miranda," I said, "you are to say nothing of what you saw to anybody. Not Father, not Aunt Sukey, not Dippity. Do you understand?"

She eyed me slyly. "And Kit?"

I wanted to slap her. "Especially not Kit!" I said.

A slow smile crept across her face. "Patience, I do believe you still have eyes for Kit!"

"I do not!" I replied hotly. "I am just afraid he will tell Father! Now promise!"

I truly believe that was the reason I did not want her to tell Kit. I do not have, as she puts it, eyes for him. But he is my friend and I do not wish to hurt him.

FRIDAY JULY 9TH

I must have convinced Miranda I do not want Kit for myself. Aunt Sukey has complained about her chasing after him. I was by the bedroom window when I heard her speak harshly to Kit this afternoon.

"That girl is no good for you," she said, "and you must not let her loiter around your master's yard. You are there to work and to learn, not dally with flirty girls."

He replied firmly but politely, and his words cheered me.

"I do not encourage her, Mistress," he said. "She is like a wasp around a fallen apple. She will not give up. And it is hardly my fault." He paused. "I do not want her."

Aunt Sukey's voice softened. "I know, boy. I know what you want. But you must have patience."

He smiled. "I must."

That set me to thinking. Here was a young man my

father likes, Aunt Sukey likes – in fact, everybody likes Kit. I do, too, a lot. But I cannot get those wickedly sparkling eyes and those insistent lips out of my mind – or my heart.

Is there any hope that, in time, I could show Father that Jeremy is right for me? I fear not.

Oh, he is so exciting! And how proud I shall be when I watch my first play and see my lover on stage.

TUESDAY JULY 13TH

The weather has been quite miserable for two days, with London looking grey and dull. When the rain eased today, I took Tiny a chicken-and-ham pasty to share with her family. She was standing by her wall, for it was too wet to sit, and had not been given much more than a penny and a half all day.

Actually, the pasty was not my idea. Dippity thought of it while she and I were baking, and we made an extra one.

Tiny was so thrilled with the gift that I am glad I did it, and I vowed that I will think of other people more often. I almost made myself laugh when I made the vow. Me? Think of other people? I do, already! If my family only knew that I think of Jeremy de la Motte constantly... I dread to think of the consequences. But I cannot help it. I think of him before I go to sleep and I think of him when I wake.

"Why's you smiling?" Tiny asked.

"I am thinking of someone," I replied.

After leaving Tiny, I met Miranda and her mother on their way back from the apothecary. Mistress Coverley has toothache again – the poor woman does suffer so – and needed some henbane. She did not stay to talk, and left us together.

Miranda was so pleased to see me, for nothing seems to be happening in London town on this damp day, and it is all misery in her home.

We talked of this and that, and then she said, "You are still keeping company with the player?"

I made a face. "I cannot call it 'keeping company', because it is difficult to find time to be together."

She smiled. "Your father would not approve, and your aunt…!"

I glared at her. "You promised you would not tell!"

"Of course not," she replied, with wide, innocent eyes.

I wish I could trust her, but I cannot.

THURSDAY JULY 15TH

I am right not to trust that scheming, artful, slug-brained baggage! Not content with lurking around Kit all the time, she has even tried to take Jeremy from me! Must she have everything I have?

Kit told me. He was not intending to, I am sure, but he seemed so uncomfortable today when he came to mend a broken stair for Father. Everyone was out and we fell to talking. He asked if I still went to the playhouse.

"When I can," I said. "It is exciting there, and it cannot be long before the first play will be performed. I have seen the costumes."

He laughed. "I have, too. It seems all the men wore some sort of dress in the time of Julius Caesar!"

"They must have done," I said. "I have even seen Master Shakespeare himself adorned in white folds."

"It's hard to tell the men's parts from the women's," Kit said. "Your friend makes a beautiful wife for Caesar."

"A handsome wife, indeed," I corrected him.

He paused in his work of rubbing the new step smooth.

"What is it?" I asked.

He looked down. "'Tis nothing. Just ... nothing."

I gripped his arm. "What? Tell me. Tell me now," I commanded. "Look at me and tell me."

He looked away, but I pulled him round to face me. "If you have something to say to me, Kit Hamble, say it now or get away from me and never speak to me again."

He drew a breath. "Your friends," he said. "Master de la Motte and ... and Miranda."

My stomach clenched. "What? What of them?"

"I saw them, Patience," said Kit. "Together."

Everything around me dimmed. All I could see were his brown eyes as I stared into them. "You lie!" I said. Then I shrieked at him. "You *lie!*"

He shook his head. "I would never lie to you, Patience. You should know that. I would never hurt you. That's why I didn't want to say anything."

He reached for my hand, but I snatched it away. "Don't touch me!" I cried. "Get out! Get out now!"

He glanced at the stair and shrugged.

"Very well, stay," I said. "I will go."

I turned on my heel and swept out of the door, slamming it behind me. Unfortunately, I slammed it so hard and so fast that my hem caught in it and I had to open it again so I could yank it free.

Curse Miranda! I hate her. How could she do this? She cannot leave any boy – any *man* alone. I always thought her a flirt, but she is sly, too.

MONDAY JULY 19TH

Miranda has not been near me for an age, but I do not read anything into that – lately I often do not see her for days on end. I haven't spoken to Kit for a while, either, and nor do I intend to. I also have not had an opportunity to go to the playhouse, which infuriates me.

However, Dippity is having to finish the hanging for the Roman play, *Julius Caesar,* very quickly, as it is the first play that will be performed. As soon as it's ready, we will take it to the Globe. The hanging has not taken nearly as long as usual, for there is only the eagle to do. Apparently, it is a symbol of Rome. Dippity can be extra quick because, as it will not be seen too closely by the play-goers, it can have large stitches. But even that is not quick enough for me, so I have been helping her, but only where the work needs filling in. She does not trust me with the outline. I cannot blame her, but I have learned that large stitches make sewing a lot more interesting, because you see the results sooner. And if you screw up your eyes, it looks quite realistic.

THURSDAY JULY 22ND

Dippity says the eagle hanging will be finished before dark tonight. Huzzah! We can take it to the playhouse tomorrow. And I shall see Jeremy.

FRIDAY JULY 23RD

I could not help myself. The moment I managed to steal a few minutes with Jeremy, I told him what Kit had said and asked if it were true.

"There is a grain of truth in what he said," Jeremy told me. My heart plummeted.

"But I did not kiss her," he went on. "She wished to whisper something to me – I forget what – and I leaned down to hear. After she had spoken, she kissed me. Just here."

He touched his finger to the corner of his mouth. I felt weak with longing. I stretched up and kissed him there myself.

"There," I said. "Was not that kiss – given with love – worth a hundred of Miranda's careless kisses?"

He glanced over my shoulder. "Someone comes."

I drew away. The back of my neck seemed to prickle. After a moment, I turned to see Kit and my father. I do not know whose face was darkest.

"Patience!" said Father. "Get you gone. And take Dippity with you. I do not wish my daughters to linger around – *players* – any longer than is necessary."

I glanced at Jeremy. His eyebrows were raised, no doubt at the way my father spat the word "players", but he did not seem concerned.

I was ashamed at my father's behaviour towards a well-bred young man.

WEDNESDAY JULY 28TH

I am cooped up indoors on Father's orders, and *so* unhappy. What must Jeremy think of me? How could he imagine that I might make a good wife for him when my father has insulted him. What must he think of my family?

Even though I cannot wander out at will, I planned to see Jeremy and put things right when I go to do my scribe work at the Globe. But I am even denied that. There is no work. All is done and the scrivener's shoulder is almost well again.

I do not wish the man ill, but if he could just hurt it a little once more it would please me.

Oh, Patience, what are you becoming? How could you ill-wish a poor, innocent man?

WEDNESDAY AUGUST 11TH

For nearly three miserable weeks I have been confined to the house. I cannot begin to describe how tedious the days are. I look out of the windows and see people chatting and laughing and going where they want. Aunt Sukey has worked me until my hands are sore and aching. I have read my mother's Bible and prayer book at least ten times over. Well, that is an exaggeration, for nobody could read *every* part of the Bible, but I have found and read all the stories, which I now know by heart.

Today I was allowed writing materials again. While I have spent so much time alone, I have been able to recall some of Master Shakespeare's lines. Saying phrases over and over to myself has allowed me to see the beauty in them that men talk about. I wonder, could I write like that? Could I write a poem, perhaps?

I immediately began to try. It was to be about love, but

my brain is so full of nothing that words would not come, and I ended up with half the first line only. But I would like to do more. Can women write plays? I don't know why not. My brain is as good, if not better, than many of the boys I grew up with.

Dippity has been kind and has sung to me – she has a sweet voice, but when she forgets the words she makes up the rest of the song and sometimes it is so funny that I have to stuff my fist in my mouth so she does not see me laugh.

She has played draughts and chess with me, and I have let her win often. But when we play at cards, I have to work to win. Dippity might have trouble remembering all sorts of things, but she has an excellent memory for cards. Yesterday she won every game except the last, and I swear she let me win that.

I do love her so much.

THURSDAY AUGUST 12TH

Miranda visited this morning, and Aunt Sukey called me and said I might go down and speak with her, but I said I had a bad head. I do not want to spend time with Miranda. I have a terrible fear that she might have been after Jeremy, and by now he might have given in and kissed her or even fallen in love with her. I cannot bear the thought and I would rather not know.

Instead I wrote some more of my poem. It is four lines long now, but I have scratched out about forty more in my efforts to make it better. Having seen Master Shakespeare's own manuscripts, I know that crossing out and trying again is something even the best writers do.

FRIDAY AUGUST 13TH

I was spreading fresh rushes on the floor this morning when Kit came in.

"I do not see you much these days, Patience," he said.

I glared at him. He cannot pretend not to know that Father had forbidden me to go out.

"Would you sit with me while I eat my pasty?" he asked.

I was about to give him another glare when I thought to myself that if I did sit with him, and if Father was watching, he might think I had given up thoughts of my Jeremy.

As we sat in the garden beneath the hollyhocks, there was a bang at the front door. Aunt Sukey was out so I went to see who it was.

"Master Shakespeare!" I said.

"Good day to you, Patience," he said. "We have missed you at the Globe. I hope you are coming to see our first play. You will recognize many of the lines, because you have written them out."

"I would very much like to see the play, sir," I said. "I so enjoyed reading the lines. In fact, I have been writing a poem and I think I would like to write a play."

"Then why do you not do so?"

"Oh, I have not the time," I said, then added hastily, "but I have the time to see your play, sir!"

"Then seats will be reserved for your family."

He went on to ask for Father, and I invited him to sit down and fetched him a cup of ale. Then I called Father from the yard.

Master Shakespeare asked him in front of me if he would bring us all to the first play. Father could hardly say no! Then he said that he was going home to Stratford in a few weeks. His sister Joan is likely to marry, and he wanted Father to make something special for her as a marriage gift.

I sat nearby in case they needed anything, and my thoughts wandered. Soon I will be back at the Globe, and I will see Jeremy, even if it is only on the stage.

WEDNESDAY SEPTEMBER 1ST

I have been to my first proper play! We went in wherries, and the river was so busy we felt in danger of crashing into other boats the whole time.

It was exciting to see two flags flying from the top of the Globe. One showed a Roman god with a globe of the world on his shoulders, and the other was bright red, which I knew, because Jeremy had told me, meant the play was to be a history play. *Julius Caesar!*

The area outside the playhouse was transformed. Stalls had been put up everywhere, and barrows, too, selling every sort of food you can imagine. There were pies and pasties and tarts, and nuts and fruit and cakes and ale, and the noise! Such a bustle!

We queued at the door and watched people putting their pennies in the box. Some paid more and collected a cushion to sit on. When we reached the door, the box man recognized Father, Dippity and me, and said, "Master Shakespeare and Master Burbage have set aside seats for you, sir. Go on in. There is nothing to pay."

Aunt Sukey looked very impressed!

There were indeed seats waiting for us. Good ones, too, with cushions ready and waiting.

I explained to Father and Aunt Sukey that the people without seats, who stood talking and eating around the yard in front of the stage, were known as groundlings. "Master Burbage said that by the end of the play they will be known as stinkards, because they will become hot and smelly," I said.

Father laughed. Aunt Sukey pretended not to have heard.

I imagined (and it turned out I was right) that the yard would be a mess after the play, because people were dropping fruit cores and nut shells just where they stood. There was such a smell of oranges, which are the most popular fruit among the poorer people. I suppose, whatever the state of their teeth, anyone can suck an orange.

We, like the groundlings, watched rich people in gorgeous clothing make their way to the Lords' rooms, and then, when it seemed that the playhouse would burst if even one more person came in, three trumpet blasts blew from the little hut on the roof.

And then the play! Oh, it is nothing like the scraps of rehearsal that I have seen before, with all the squabbling and laughter and interruptions.

No, this was – I do not know how to express it. It was something perfect. We were in Rome – and there was the hanging that Dippity and I had stitched – and how Father enjoyed it when one of the first men on stage turned out to be playing a carpenter!

"It is an old trade indeed!" he said to Aunt Sukey.

I recognized many of the words spoken, for I had copied them out for the players. It made me feel important, though it was annoying that hardly anyone there knew it. Occasionally food sellers came over to the people in our row, offering us things to eat and drink, but we had no appetite. Aunt Sukey had made us eat well before we left home.

"We must not waste money on food, when we have all we need here," she had said.

During the time my love was on stage my chest felt so tight I could barely breathe. I sensed Father looking at me a couple of times, but I kept my face straight, hoping I was not flushed.

All I could think as I watched Jeremy move about the stage in the feminine way that was so unlike his usual manner was, "I love that man."

I had seen many parts being rehearsed, so I knew what to expect, but poor Aunt Sukey didn't. When Julius Caesar was stabbed, with very much blood, she turned pale.

I laughed. "It is a trick, Aunt," I said, but when I explained that the players had pigs' bladders filled with blood hidden in their costumes, she said it made her feel sick.

Shortly after the stabbing, an apple woman appeared beside Father, who waved her away. But she held out an apple, saying, "These are gifts for friends of the Chamberlain's Men." When I received my apple, I felt something else in my hand. I was confused and put my hands in my lap. I did not have a chance to look to see what it was, because I was sitting so close to Father on one side, and to Dippity on the other. She would surely have exclaimed and asked what it was if she had seen it.

I knew what I hoped it would be.

I hardly noticed the rest of the play. I certainly did not eat my apple. As we started home, I clutched the folded piece of paper in my closed hand, feeling the warmth coming from it.

Only when I was in the bedroom did I unfold it and read it by the light from the window.

It said, "I hope you are enjoying my performance." It was signed J de l M, and finished with a roughly drawn heart shape.

I do not remember ever being so disappointed. But he did draw a heart.

THURSDAY SEPTEMBER 2ND

I saw him! I saw him today!

I was bringing a duck home from market and, as I

passed Tiny, sheltering from the sun beneath her shawl, I tried to make her laugh by holding up the duck and quacking loudly at her.

She smiled.

Just then I noticed a tall figure striding up from the river. Jeremy!

He saw me and, as that wonderful smile spread across his face, I thought, *He is glad to see me.*

I ran around the corner, so that Tiny would not see us together and, in a moment, he appeared. I ran into his arms, and we slipped into an alley between the cobbler's and a cookshop.

I dropped the duck and he kissed me lightly before we spoke. And I learned that Master Shakespeare had told him to leave me alone, because my father does not approve of him.

"I confess I am surprised," he said, stroking my neck with a fingertip. "A young man of good family being rejected by a mere carpenter? I may be a player, but that is through choice, through love of poetry, not out of necessity."

I was mortified. I was torn between anger that he had been insulted, and anguish that my father had been spoken of with such derision.

He drew away from me a little, and the thought flew into my mind that, because of my father, he would not want me any more.

But he simply looked down at me and said, "And am I

also to be rejected by the carpenter's daughter?"

I put my hands on his shoulders. "You are not! You are not!" I cried. "But it is all so difficult. There is Father, and Miranda, who I do not trust, and even Kit, who was my dear friend – they all think I should not see you."

He pressed himself against me, and even though my heart seemed to be pounding in my chest, I could feel the steady beat of my love's heart, too.

"Do you truly care for me, Patience?" he murmured in my ear.

"You know I do."

"Then meet me tomorrow," he said, urgently. "We will spend some time – together."

"But I am afraid we will be seen," I said.

He nibbled my earlobe. "Come to my lodgings," he said. "Tomorrow."

I wanted nothing more.

"I can't," I said, and he groaned. "Not tomorrow, but the next day. Aunt Sukey is going to visit her sister, who has cut her leg badly. Father is going with her to replace some broken floorboards. That is how she cut her leg."

He relaxed and smiled. "I will meet you when the church bell strikes ten," he said.

"Where?" I asked.

"Here, around the corner from the church," he said.

I nodded happily, and left him.

"Patience!" he called, and I turned expectantly.

He grinned and pointed to the feathery heap on the ground. "You forgot your duck!"

Oh, I cannot wait for Saturday. I long to see his London lodging. It will be small, of course, because it is for only one person. It will be cosy.

SATURDAY SEPTEMBER 4TH

This morning Father brought the barrow round to the front door, and Aunt Sukey piled all sorts of goodies on top of Father's tools.

"Some raspberries!" she cried. "I must pick some raspberries for her!"

"I will get them," I said, and grabbed a bowl. I knew I would be quicker, and I could not wait for them to leave. I'd heard the nine o'clock bell long before and I needed to change out of my house clothes.

At last they were gone, and I was ready. I left Dippity cutting herbs to dry. I told her I was going to look in the market for some ribands, and that I might linger awhile with Miranda and her mother if I should see them. Of course, I hoped I would not!

The weather was warm and sunny, with a strong breeze, and I took my light cloak, so I could cover myself if I chanced to see anyone I knew. And who was the first person I saw? Or rather heard?

"Patience!" Miranda called from her window. "Wait! I will accompany you!"

That was the very last thing I wanted. "No!" I cried. "I am going to meet – a friend."

"Who? *Who?*"

"It is not your business to know," I called up.

"Jeremy!" she said. "You are going to meet Jeremy. I know you are!"

Indeed, she did not look pleased.

"No, I am..." I began, but she vanished from her window.

I turned and walked straight into Kit, who was taking a sack of sawdust to the butcher. I had forgotten that Father lets him gather and sell the sawdust on a Saturday, and keep the money for himself. *Mercy me*, I thought, *is there no peace from people interfering in my life?*

I said hello and goodbye to him, then raced down the street until I reached the corner by the church.

I know I am becoming a better person because, in spite of my anxiety to see Jeremy, I had thought to take a piece of gingerbread for Tiny. She was in her usual place. She greeted me with a smile and took the gingerbread from me with many thanks. She pulled the cloth from it and held it with her bad hand, while she broke off a piece with her good one.

"Bless you, Mistress Patience," she said, with her mouth full, then the poor creature coughed, spraying gingerbread crumbs everywhere. She should not be coughing like that in summer.

I was mindful that Miranda was probably looking for me, and indeed when I looked through the throng of people in the street, I spotted her bright hair in the sunlight as she talked to someone. A horse's head obscured their faces, so I could not see who it was. At least, I thought, it meant she had probably forgotten me.

I said farewell to Tiny and hurried around the corner. To my delight, Jeremy was leaning against a wall, looking so tall and elegant and handsome that my breath caught in my throat.

I ran to him and he swept me into his arms. Then he took my hand and led me down towards the river. We turned right and followed it past fish sellers and oyster women, and the wonderful scents from a spice merchant's warehouse. Eventually we turned right again, away from the water.

In just a short while Jeremy led me along a narrow passage that widened out into a damp court where the sun did not reach. Doors led into the buildings to left and right. Chickens in wooden boxes stood against the walls, and in the far corner was a pig in a stinking pen. Filthy water ran along the cobbles down the middle of the court.

I clung to Jeremy as a ragged old woman crept past, muttering to herself.

"What is this place?" I asked. "Is this where you live?"

He must have heard the disbelief in my voice. "It is but a place to rest my head," he said. "It is not what I would choose, but Thomas's family own this building and he offered me a room. I agreed before I saw it, and if I had then refused it, it would have seemed as if I was a little – above myself." He smiled. "I spend most of my spare time at the home of my sister and her husband in The Strand."

He looked down at me. "Is it not good enough for you?"

I hesitated. I did not want him to think I was like my father, thinking myself superior. "Of course it is good enough," I said, "but it's a lovely day. Why don't we stay outside in the fresh air?"

He grinned and pulled me to him. "Let's go inside. I want to show you how much I love you. I cannot do that here. Not with the pig watching."

That made me laugh. It also made me feel a little more relaxed. I knew from Miranda's experiences that I must be careful when alone with a man, but I also knew I would be safe with Jeremy. I leaned against him, and felt him reach out to open the door.

It was then that I thought I must be seeing things. I was facing the dingy passage that was the entrance to the court, and the sunlight beyond was bright. A figure was standing looking down towards us, and it took a moment or two for my eyes to adjust enough to allow me to recognize him. For a "him" it was.

"Kit!" I whispered. "It's Kit."

I was appalled – not that he should find me with Jeremy, but that he should find me in such a low place. And I was angry! There was no reason for him to be around that district. He had followed me. I was sure of it.

"Patience!" he shouted. "Come away. Come away now."

"Jeremy, it is Kit," I moaned. "He has followed me."

"He is nothing," said my love. "Never mind him. He has company of his own. See?"

Only then did I realize there was another figure silhouetted against the sunlight.

Miranda! She must have told Kit what I was doing and followed us. Of course! I had seen her talking to someone, but a horse's head was in the way. The horse must have been Blossom and she'd been speaking to Kit! How could I not recognize our own horse?

"Come inside," Jeremy said, his hand gripping my wrist.

But I was scared. "Kit will tell my father."

"Is your father a violent man?" he asked me.

"No. Not violent. He is a gentle man."

Jeremy slipped into the doorway and pulled me after him. I tried to resist.

"Come in," he said, and his voice was not so gentle now. "Even if he tells your father, it will be a while before they return. We can have that time together. Come," he urged.

"No," I said, and I know I was whimpering. "Jeremy, I am afraid."

"Patience! Come away!" Kit shouted again. "If you do not, I will fetch your father."

Jeremy stroked my arms from my shoulders to my wrists, then hugged me. "If your father is not a violent man, he probably would not beat you," he said softly. "So why fear him? We shall be here just a few minutes, no longer, I promise, and then you can be gone and you can swear the boy made a mistake."

I began to panic. "No, I must go," I said. "Let me go!" I cried, for he was holding me too tightly.

"Stay with me," he urged. "Just a while, my sweet, that's all I want."

Jeremy was almost lifting me further into that horrible hovel.

I struggled. "No! Please! I must go and speak to Kit. I must stop him. Let me go! *Let me go!*"

He pushed me aside, but gripped one of my wrists tightly. I looked into his face. It seemed darkened.

"Go after your carpenter's boy," he said angrily. "But you are a fool. No one would take his word above yours."

"They will!" I wrenched my wrist free and whirled

around, heading out into the stinking court and towards the dark passage. "Everybody likes him," I shouted over my shoulder. "Everybody trusts him! Kit!" I called. "I'm coming! No – wait!" For as soon as he saw me coming towards him, he turned away and disappeared from view. I suppose he felt his job was done.

Jeremy ran after me. "See?" he said, as he caught me by the arm. "He has gone. He is not bothered." He tucked a stray strand of hair behind my ear. "He doesn't care for you, Patience, not like I do."

Oh, when he looked at me with such passion in his eyes, I was so torn. But I knew I must go after Kit. I must stop him causing trouble with Father.

"If I cannot stop Kit telling tales, Father will keep me indoors for *ever*!" I cried. "I would never see you again!"

Once more I wrenched myself free and raced up the passage. I had to catch up with Kit and persuade him to say nothing.

I turned into the street, and there stood Miranda, leaning against a wall, smirking.

I swore at her, then ran like I had never run before. My mind was whirling. I prayed that I had not upset Jeremy so much that he wouldn't want to see me again. *I could not bear that*, I thought. *I could not bear it if he left my life.*

As I raced around the church corner I almost fell against Kit. He was bending over Tiny, lifting her gently into his arms.

He saw me, but acted as if I was invisible.

I barely had the breath to speak. "What is wrong with her?" I gasped. Her grubby little face looked only half awake.

He turned and looked at me. "She must have fallen asleep. One leg was sticking out and I fell over it. I'm going to buy some food and take her back to her family." He looked up at the sky where clouds were building up. "It will rain before long."

"I will come with you," I said.

"No," he said. "Go home, Patience. For God's sake, go home."

I wanted to slap him for ordering me about, but common sense stopped me. I needed Kit on my side. I tucked Tiny's shawl around her, then said, "Please may we speak before ... before..."

"Before your father gets home, I suppose?" he said. "I have nothing to say to you, Patience."

He walked away, carrying Tiny as if she weighed no more than a feather pillow. I don't suppose she does.

Me? I did as Kit said, and came home.

LATER

I have been writing by the window but the evening is cloudy and the light is almost gone. I have lit a candle, and it feels as if the little flame is the only warmth in my life.

Dippity was out when I arrived home. The only movement in the house was from Aunt Sukey's spiteful cat.

I ran upstairs and sat on the window seat, watching the rain. I could not believe I had taken orders from my father's apprentice. What right does he have to tell me what to do? I grew angry. I was in such a bad state and it was his fault. Kit had left me agitated, so agitated, because I did not know what he would decide to do.

Maybe, I thought, I could speak to Father first and tell him Kit is always following me, and keeps making up stories about me.

No. Nobody who knows him would believe that, least of all my father.

I sat brooding until, after a while, I saw Kit walk past the house and round the corner. I guessed he was heading for the yard. A few minutes later, there was a knock on the back door. I leaned out of the upstairs window and called,

"Come in." Then I ran down the stairs and stood while he removed his boots and tossed his head to shake the water off. His hair looked so glittery, covered in raindrops.

"Why did you follow me?" I demanded. Then, without giving him time to answer, I said, "You were spying on me!"

"I was trying to keep you safe!"

"You have no right!"

He laughed scornfully. "Patience, in that situation, I think I had every right. I wished to protect my master's daughter. And that I have done. You are a fool. Can you possibly not realize what was going to happen to you if you went inside that – that filthy hovel?"

I changed my approach. "Have some ale while we talk," I said, and fetched the jug and a cup. Once he settled at the table to drink, I sat on the bench opposite and said meekly, "Please don't tell Father."

He put the cup down with a thump. "Why not?"

"Because I have done nothing wrong," I said. "Well, nothing very wrong."

He glared. "That is only thanks to me. Who knows what state you would have been in if you'd let de la Motte have his way. How could he *think* of taking you there? He cannot possibly live there, not someone of his standing."

I had to defend my lover. "He sleeps there rather than offend someone who is less well off than him," I said. "I call that a gentlemanly way to behave."

He was silent, staring into his ale.

I reached out and touched his hand. "Thanks to you, Kit, I was strong enough to walk away from him," I said. "And I'm glad I did," I lied. At least, I think I lied. I really hadn't wanted to go into that building, but I so wanted to be with Jeremy. I still do.

It seemed a good idea to keep quiet then, and to leave my fingertips just touching the roughness of Kit's hand. Jeremy's hands are pale and clean. Soft on my skin.

Suddenly, Kit looked up. "Patience, I will say nothing this time," he said. I cast my eyes down. "Thank you, Kit," I said, as meekly as I could manage.

"This time, I said."

"Yes, Kit." I was so relieved, I felt tears spring to my eyes.

When he stood up to go, he took me by my shoulders and shook me. "Patience, you must take care. He is no good for you. Give him up! Swear to me now that you will have nothing more to do with him."

I didn't move. I couldn't.

He let go of me, went to the shelf and fetched the Bible. He put it on the table, took my hand and laid it on top. "Swear!"

I looked down at the book. It was my mother's.

I shook my head. "No."

"Yes. Swear!"

"I cannot," I wailed. "I love him!"

Kit stepped back, looking as if I had slapped him. He slumped down on the bench.

"For God's sake, Patience," he said. "He's a player. You surely know what sort of people players are? Master Shakespeare and Master Burbage and one or two others excepted," he added, "though heaven knows, even they are not without reproach."

"Kit," I said, and I hated myself for sounding so pleading, "he is a good man, from a good family. He acts for the love of it, for the poetry of it. He has such a sensitive soul."

"Pah! Players act for the money, not for love."

I had him there. "Jeremy does not need money. The de la Motte family is wealthy, as you well know." I heard someone at the gate. "He just has to prove to his father that he is doing something worthy. He said when he is one of the owners of the Chamberlain's Men, he will tell his father the truth about what he is doing."

Kit snorted. "*I'd* like to tell his father."

"Oh, you must not even think of such a thing!" I said. But as the de la Mottes live miles and miles away in Huntingdonshire there is little chance of that happening.

The door opened and in came Dippity. She looked tired, damp and bedraggled, and she fell into my arms.

"Oh, Patience, you are safe," she cried. "You were gone so long I was worried. I went to look for you. I got lost and it rained." She buried her face in her hands. "Frightened!"

113

I was ashamed. When I'd arrived home, I had not even thought to check to see if she was all right.

Kit took her shawl and hung it in front of the fire. "See, Patience, what trouble you cause?"

As Dippity went upstairs to change into dry clothes, I heard voices outside. A moment later in came Father and Aunt Sukey.

I felt panicked. Even though Kit had said he would not tell, could I be sure he would keep his word?

"Welcome home!" I said. "I hope you are not too wet. Dippity is upstairs and I was just giving Kit some refreshment. Let me get some for you. How is your dear sister, Aunt Sukey? I hope she is better. Father, did you manage to mend—"

They were all staring at me.

I forced a laugh. "Sorry, I am gabbling," I said. "I have spent too much of the day alone."

Kit's eyes met mine. I smiled, but he did not return my smile.

I hope he still likes me, a bit. He is cross about Dippity. I can't do anything right in his eyes. But I don't care, as long as he stays quiet.

MONDAY SEPTEMBER 6TH

I am in torment. I want to be with Jeremy, but everyone is so against him, and I am afraid they will all turn against me, too. This morning I took a chance when Aunt Sukey was out buying material for a new kirtle. She always takes an age, as she can never decide on a colour, so I slipped out, thinking I might go to Jeremy's lodging and see if he was there. Perhaps I could make everything all right.

When I reached Tiny's corner, she held out her good hand towards me. I took it, and her little face looked up at me.

"Your friend," she said. "The kind one. He carried me till we met one of me sisters. My grandfather wants me to thank 'im. He is a good young man."

"Kit, you mean?" I said. "I will tell him."

She coughed, then when the spasm had passed, she looked up, but her attention was caught by someone behind me. "That nosy old woman's coming down the street," she said, "the one what lives near you and knows everyone's business."

Goody Trickett! She is one of those people who recounts

every moment of her day, and if she got talking to Aunt Sukey, my movements would no longer be a secret.

"Good morrow," I said, as she drew near.

"And where are you off to so early, Patience Whittingham," she said, ignoring Tiny. "What are you up to? Does your aunt know where you are?"

"She does not," I replied. "I have been into the church to say a prayer for a dear friend. And now I have a headache, so I must go home. Good day, Mistress Trickett." I waved to Tiny, who was coughing, whether from illness or laughter I could not be sure.

Hoping God would forgive me for yet another lie, I hurried back up towards the house. I had to forget about Jeremy for today.

I also forgot all about Kit, until this moment. As I look from the window, I can see him using a brace and bit to drill holes in a thick piece of wood. He is a hard worker. Even when Father is not there, he is never lazy.

WEDNESDAY SEPTEMBER 8TH

Aunt Sukey is not well. She seems tired much of the time, probably because she goes to help her sister each day. This afternoon she went to lie on her bed for a while, and I soon heard her snores.

I slipped out and walked straight into Mistress Coverley, coming to ask Aunt Sukey for some eggs. I said my aunt was asleep and fetched her the eggs.

She asked where I was going. I had no idea – I just wanted to be out. I told her I was off to a little shop close to the river where they sell the prettiest ribands and laces, and the woman does not mind you looking and not buying.

"Take Miranda with you," she said. "She has been in a fret all morning because I made her scrub the floors. I should like a break from her company."

Miranda was the last person I wanted to be with, but it would have invited questions if I had said that. So, in minutes, she and I were walking in an uncomfortable silence towards the Thames.

The weather was still and warm and, when we reached the shop, I fancied I could hear laughter coming from one or other of the playhouses over on the south bank. There was a white flag flying above the Globe, which meant they were performing a comedy. It would be *The Taming of the Shrew* or *A Midsummer Night's Dream*, which I long to see. I have watched rehearsals for a scene with the queen of the fairies (not my Jeremy) and a man with an ass's head, and I think it would be very funny. That made me smile.

Suddenly I found myself alone. I quickly put down the

butter-yellow braid I had been examining, and looked round for Miranda.

There she was, almost at the riverbank, laughing and tossing her head and flirting with three young men who were so brown from the sun that they must have recently come from a ship.

I wandered near, and was about to try to attract her attention when a hand waving wildly from a wherry attracted my attention.

Jeremy! My heart sang! I didn't care who saw me. I hitched up my petticoats and raced down to the landing steps.

The wherryman rowed in – oh, so slowly! – and Jeremy was standing even before it touched the side. He thrust a coin at the man and leapt up the steps into my arms.

"I'm sorry, I'm sorry that I went after Kit that day," I cried. "I was afraid. I wanted to be with you, but—"

He put his finger against my lips. "Hush," he said. "That was a different day, and it is past." Then he kissed me, slow and hard.

"Are you not in a play today?" I asked, when he released me.

He scowled. "There is no part for me this afternoon. But tomorrow I am Beatrice, in a new play called *Much Ado About Nothing*. It is the biggest female part, and Burbage and Shakespeare have promised that if I do well I shall take men's parts from now on."

"That is good news," I said.

"And I will do well," he said. "It is an excellent part. I will be the best in the play."

"I am glad you are not acting today," I said.

"I am going home to make sure my words are perfect for tomorrow," he said, and moved even closer to me.

I suddenly remembered where we were. "This place is too public, and Miranda is nearby."

He pushed me against a wall, and wrapped himself around me, burying his face in my neck. His dark curls tickled my face as he kissed me with tiny little kisses that barely touched my skin.

"There," he murmured, "you are so small in my arms that no one can see who you are."

I told him I thought he had forgotten me.

He laughed. "Forget you? How could I?" He ran his hands down my back and pressed me to him. "We will carry on just as before, Patience. Will you come to my lodging again? Poor as it is? And stay this time? I would take you to meet my family, but it is too far. Maybe in the winter time when I am not so busy at the playhouse."

I realized then that he does care for me. He would not introduce me to his family if he was not serious.

But it is impossible.

"Jeremy, it is so difficult to be with you. Father does not want me to be with a player. Even Master Shakespeare told him it is not a good thing."

He drew his head back. "Did he, indeed?"

"And I know that Kit watches me. He could easily find out that I'm with you and it's certain he would tell Father next time." An awful thought came into my mind. "And Father might tell Master Shakespeare, then if he is disapproving, you would not get the acting parts you want!"

Jeremy pressed his lips together. "And it is all Kit. A carpenter's boy."

Oh, what a confusion. Now I feel mean because I have made Jeremy hate Kit, when I do know that Kit would never intend to hurt me – he believes he watches me for my own good.

I looked into those beautiful dark eyes. "Will you leave me now?" I asked.

He grinned. "I don't give in that easily," he said. "All will be well, you'll see."

"Patience! Is that *you*?" came Miranda's voice.

I quickly pushed my love away and straightened my bodice as she strode towards us.

"You secretive hussy!" she said, but I noticed her eyes were on Jeremy. Was it my imagination, or did something unspoken flit between them? I remembered her staying by the dark passage when I ran away from Jeremy and after Kit.

"Miranda, if you—" I began, but Jeremy was looking directly at her, right into her eyes.

"You won't say anything, Miranda," he said. "Will you?"

She looked up at him and shook her head. I swear she blushed.

He blew me a kiss, called, "Remember, all will be well," and was gone.

Miranda and I watched him until he disappeared, then turned for home.

"He has beautiful eyes," she said, glancing back.

That witch had better keep her own eyes off him.

TUESDAY SEPTEMBER 14TH

Father and Kit have been working at the playhouse again, and I hate them for it. I want to be there. They are working on a throne for the play about Henry the Fifth. They thought it was done, but the company have decided it did not look grand enough on stage, and needs to be taller at the back, with more fancy carving or something. I suppose the groundlings at the front, by the stage, can see it very close to, so it has to look as if it belongs to a king.

This afternoon, Kit came back early. I saw him lead Blossom into the yard as I was taking some cabbage leaves to the chickens.

"What are you doing?" I called, as he unhitched the horse.

"Why have you brought the throne back? Where is Father?"

"He wants to put the final touches to it here," he replied. "I think he's tired of people watching over his shoulder and offering advice."

He led Blossom to a bucket of water and left her to drink.

"That does not explain why you are back so early," I said, but I smiled, in case he thought me abrupt. In truth, I was sharp with him because I was feeling cross, being stuck in the house when I want to be somewhere else. With someone else.

He went to the back of the cart and hefted his tool bag into his arms. He is very muscular.

"Master Whittingham stayed to have a drink with Master Burbage," he said. "I cannot help him with that. When he returns, I shall help him with the throne. In the meantime, I am to put a new leg on Mistress Sukey's little fireside stool, and a new roof on your henhouse."

I giggled. "The chickens do look a little bedraggled in the morning when it has rained in the night!"

He smiled. "Best get on then. Stool first, or henhouse first?"

"Who would you rather please?" I asked. "Aunt Sukey or the chickens?"

Before he could reply, Aunt Sukey's voice floated from her open window. "I heard that!"

He grinned. "The stool it is!"

Kit is so nice when he is not all anxious and stressed. Or angry.

I offered to fetch him a bowl of chicken broth, and he came inside and dumped his tool bag on the floor, then turned the stool over to examine it. He rummaged in the bag for a tool, which he used to poke around the hole left by the broken leg.

"I had better do this in the yard," he said. "Mistress Whittingham will not like wood shavings all over her floor."

"Have your broth first," I said, putting it on the table with a wedge of warm fresh bread.

As he stood up, he knocked my elbow and I dropped the spoon. It fell into his tool bag, so I went to pick it up.

"No!" he said, shoving my hand aside. "I will get it."

Did he think I was going to break his stupid tools?

As he ate, Dippity came in, carrying a huge basket of damsons.

"Where did you get all those?" I asked in dismay, for I could guess who would be taking the stones out.

"Aunt Sukey's sister," she said. "She cannot pick her fruit, because of her poor leg, so I am doing it. She gave me some sugar. We are going to make her some damson jam and a pie for us."

"We are, are *we*?" I said. That was unkind. I know she must look after her hands, because rough skin catches terribly on silks and lace.

I dished up a bowl of broth for her, and as she sat down, Kit said, "Dippity! I almost forgot. I have a message for you. Can you go to the playhouse tomorrow—"

My heart leapt.

"—and do a repair on that black hanging? One of the players caught his foot in it and it tore. There is barely any damage to your fancy stitching, but Master Burbage says they would rather pay you to do a fine job than have 'some clack-clawed clodpoll stitching it up like a surgeon sewing up wounds after a fight with blunt daggers'."

We all laughed. It felt good to laugh together.

Kit picked up his bag and went into the garden. Aunt Sukey came down and started to make the pastry while I dealt with the damsons.

Once the pastry was ready and the damsons were stewing, she glanced through the open kitchen door and saw Kit working on the henhouse.

"I thought he wanted to please me, rather than the hens," she said.

"He has," I said, pointing to the doorstep. "Look, there is your stool, ready and waiting for you."

She wiped her hands and took it from me. "Oh, he is a good lad," she said. "Thank you, Kit!" she called from the doorway.

He looked round and smiled. He really is quite handsome. In an ordinary sort of way.

124

LATER

Father has come home in a bit of a mood. "What a day!" he said, as he washed his hands and face. "There has been a theft at the playhouse and everybody suspects everybody else. Trouble is, Master Shakespeare and Master Burbage are worried that all the players will be unsettled until the thief is discovered, and not give of their best." He dried his hands. "I tell you, this is bad news."

"But what happened, Harry? What was stolen?" asked Aunt Sukey.

"A ring belonging to Master Shakespeare," said Father. "When he changed into his costume, he took the ring off, as he always does, and put it in his little box that I made him. He says he definitely locked the box, and put the key beneath the clothing which he left behind in the tiring room just before he went on stage. When he dressed after the performance, the key was where he left it, and so was the box. But the ring was gone."

Aunt Sukey looked puzzled. "Are you saying that a thief found the key, opened the box, took the ring, then carefully locked it up again and replaced the key in its hiding place?"

"Seems so." He sat down and pulled off his boots. "But when you put it like that, it does seem a bit ridiculous," he said. "Maybe the thief wanted to be sure to leave before the theft was discovered, in case he was searched. Who knows? But players are a superstitious lot, and as soon as someone said it was bad luck on a playhouse to have a thief in the company, that was it. Everyone's got themselves in a twist about it. Ay, ridiculous."

"Ridiculous indeed," said Aunt Sukey, with a sniff. "Obviously there *was* no theft. Master Shakespeare must be getting forgetful. He clearly put the ring somewhere else. Perhaps he left it in his lodgings that morning."

Father sighed. "That is probably the right explanation," he said. "But at the moment, he insists it has been stolen, and from someone who comes into the tiring room."

I spoke up then. "But only people who work for the company are allowed into the tiring room," I said. "Oh, Father, we all go into the tiring room – you and I, and Dippity!"

He smiled. "You girls are above suspicion," he said. "You were not there today."

Of course! How silly of me!

"I was there," he said, "and I was searched, like all the others. That did offend me, I must admit," he added.

I felt very glad I had not been there. Imagine being treated as a criminal, and worse, being searched!

Father yawned. "I must have something to eat, and then

I am going to my bed. Tomorrow morning I must be up with the sun and finish that wretched throne. Then Kit and I have to deliver some shields and swords to the Globe. Maybe the ring will have turned up by then. Perhaps Master Shakespeare tossed it into his box and missed? It could be lying around on the floor somewhere."

Dippity touched his hand. "Father, I am to go to the playhouse tomorrow, to make a small repair. Shall I come with you?"

He stroked her hair. "You shall, my love. And Patience, you must come, too, so you can bring your sister home safely. Kit and I will be staying awhile. We are building a bed!"

WEDNESDAY SEPTEMBER 15TH

This was a very strange and frightening day. My poor father is in despair.

Dippity and I watched Kit help Father load the finished throne on the cart. I thought how well they worked together. I felt it was because Kit respected my father, and Father respected him, even though he is only an apprentice.

Father tied the last rope, gave Blossom a gentle pat and said, "To the Globe!"

Instantly my thoughts turned to Jeremy. A wonderful warm feeling stole throughout my body and my legs felt weak. Surely, I thought, only true love could make a girl feel like that. It is wonderful. But how are we ever going to be together?

We all walked alongside the cart, so as not to strain poor Blossom. As we passed Tiny, Dippity broke away to slip a small damson pie into her hands. She had baked it specially. I wish I had thought of doing that. I had to content myself with waving and shouting, "Good day, Tiny!" She took the pie in her good hand and waved the other one to me – the one that does not work properly.

Dippity hurried back to my side. "She wants to talk to you, Patience," she said. "She says it's important."

But I couldn't wait to get to the playhouse, so I said I would go and see Tiny on the way home.

It was a beautiful morning, but a strong, cool breeze was blowing up the river, and it hit us every time we reached a gap in the buildings on the bridge. People pointed at the throne on the cart. I suggested we sit Dippity up there.

"People might think you are a mysterious princess," I told her. "They would bow or curtsy to you."

Kit laughed. "Dippity does not need to sit on a throne to look like a mysterious princess," he said, and made her a deep bow. She blushed and looked down at the ground. He took her hand, then lifted her chin and said, "I am only teasing, Dippity, but it is true that you are as pretty as a princess."

I wished he wouldn't fuss over her, because it might give her the idea that he cares for her.

Then I thought, *Perhaps he does*. And then I thought, *Suppose he does?* I lagged behind and spent the rest of the walk imagining what would happen if Kit and Dippity fell in love and got married. He would be my brother. He would be with us always. Hmm, I thought. I would like that.

But it is not to be.

We arrived at the Globe to find everyone in turmoil. Some players were trying to rehearse, but every so often a squabble would break out and accusations and insults would be hurled around. I was pleased to see that Jeremy looked calm, sitting on the edge of the stage with some other players, quietly learning his words. The weasel-faced Thomas eyed us as we came in. He did not smile, even at Father.

One of the tiring men showed Dippity what she had to do, and I went to sit on a bench where I could gaze at Jeremy, willing him to come over to me and kiss me. That was stupid, and it would not happen, not with Father there, and Dippity and, of course, Kit, who sees all.

Father and Kit had lifted the throne into the tiring room, and were just coming out when Thomas suddenly pointed and cried out, "What about him?"

He was pointing towards Father and Kit. They both stopped, looking confused.

Thomas strode towards them. "He was here yesterday,"

he said, clapping a hand on to Kit's shoulder. "He left early, did he not?"

Father replied, "He did, and what of it? He is my apprentice to command."

The player continued, "Was he searched?"

No one replied, and Thomas went on, "For the ring? Was he searched?"

"He was not," said Father. "He was not here when the ring disappeared."

Master Shakespeare moved to Father's side. "I must correct you, sir. He was not here when the theft was discovered," he said, then he turned to Kit. "You will not mind being searched, will you?"

Kit shrugged. "I have nothing to hide," he said.

And they took him into the tiring room and searched him. I can only imagine they stripped him first, because they took so long, and when they came out, Kit looked rumpled and flushed.

"Nothing, I'll wager?" said Father, looking confident.

"Nothing," said Master Shakespeare.

I breathed a sigh of relief. I knew, of course, that Kit would not steal, but it was a relief to be sure.

I went to sit back down, when Thomas's voice rang out. "What about his bag of tools?"

Kit went to pick it up, fetched it over to the watching men and opened it, holding it out for all to see.

Another player took the bag and upended it on the ground. He stirred the tools with his foot, then froze.

He bent forward, moved a mallet and picked up something that lay beneath. He held it out to Master Shakespeare.

"Your ring, Will."

There were shouts of joy and of relief. I glanced across at Jeremy. He was smiling. He was glad to see Kit in trouble.

And in trouble Kit definitely was. Father, he, Master Shakespeare and Master Burbage went into the tiring room and threw everyone out. They talked for a long time. As we waited, Dippity clasped my hand. I remembered yesterday, when I went to get the spoon I'd dropped in his tool bag. Kit had knocked my hand aside and spoken sharply to me.

As my mind whirled, Father came out of the tiring room with Kit between him and Master Burbage. As they crossed the yard, Father beckoned Dippity and me to him.

"Go home," he said. "I will join you later. I have no heart for work this day."

Indeed, he looked dreadful. His skin was grey and he looked as if he did not have the energy to stand up straight and tall.

Kit was as white as milk, and his lips were pressed together. He looked me in the eyes and said, "Patience, do not believe this of me. I did not do it."

"Shut your mouth!" said Father.

I was shocked to hear him speak like that. Dippity

gripped my arm and moved close to me. I turned and took her out, casting one last glance at my lover. He smiled at me, and blew a kiss.

I know Kit saw. He looked as if he was in pain.

THURSDAY SEPTEMBER 16TH

Father returned late yesterday. I heard him come in, and crept downstairs in my nightgown.

He was sitting at the table, with a plate of cold meat in front of him, but he just stared at it.

Aunt Sukey made a hot posset for herself and me, and we sat in silence waiting for Father to speak.

When he did, it was in a low voice. "I cannot believe it. But I have to believe it, because the proof was there."

We waited again.

"I've lost the best apprentice I ever had," he said. "And I've lost all my dreams of us building my business up together, and of being able to do the sort of woodwork I love. Now I must go back to planks and pegs."

"I am sorrier than I can say to see Kit go," said Aunt Sukey, "but you can get another apprentice, and still do your fancy work."

Father shook his head. "Kit is no ordinary woodworker. It would have been special, working with him and teaching him. No, I must get a leaden-headed boy, who I will have to watch all the time." He stared into space. "If I gave Kit a task, I could leave him to it and trust him to do it well."

I spoke then, saying something so obvious I could not understand why they had not thought of it themselves. "Father, if you believe Kit is innocent, then your problem is solved. You can keep him as your apprentice!"

He laughed, but it was not a real laugh. "Patience, you do not understand. It is only through the goodness and understanding of Master Shakespeare and Master Burbage that Kit is not locked up awaiting hanging."

"What do you mean?" asked Aunt Sukey.

"Master Shakespeare agreed that if I got rid of Kit, nothing more would be said about it. But I cannot keep him. Carpenters go into people's homes to work," he said. "We grow to be trusted by our customers. How would it be if I took a thief into some grand house? And believe me, Patience, they would soon know."

Aunt Sukey nodded. "'Tis true. A working man's good reputation is one of the most valuable things he owns. And his competitors would be the first to put him down by spreading bad news." She gasped and put her hand to her mouth. "Harry, if you took Kit back, and he stole again, you could be blamed for the theft! You might be hanged yourself!"

Father rubbed his tired face with his hands. "I know. It is impossible. I cannot keep him." He sighed. "I feel I'm letting down John Hamble."

"And Kit's mother," I said, remembering that sweet, fragile lady. "What will happen to her now? We mustn't let her starve."

Aunt Sukey stood and picked up the posset cups. "She will not starve, Patience. We will see to that. Tomorrow, you can go to her, and assure her that your father will do what he can in the circumstances to help Kit get some sort of work, and you can take a basket of goodies with you."

I wasn't sure I wanted to face Rose Hamble, but I could hardly say so.

The last thing I heard Father say as I climbed the stairs was, "Such a waste. Such a loss. For all of us."

FRIDAY SEPTEMBER 17TH

Father looks so miserable. He feels he's let his friend down, his friend's wife, and our whole family.

"With Kit working for me, I would have had someone who loved the work as much as I do," he grumbled, "and someone I could trust with my business." He paused.

"Someone I thought I could trust. And I had hoped that Patience..." He stopped.

Aunt Sukey and he looked at each other. I know what he hoped. And it makes me feel guilty. Oh, everything makes me feel guilty!

"Here, Patience," said Aunt Sukey, handing me a big basket. "There's a small cheese, a loaf of good bread, some carrots and the last of the peas. And two of my meat and potato pasties. Kit likes those."

I took the basket, and a tear ran down my cheek as I turned away. Who was I feeling sorry for? Father? Most certainly. Kit? Yes, even though he has done a bad thing and made Father unhappy. Mistress Hamble? Yes, of course. She must be very sad and worried. Myself? Well, yes, I *do* feel sorry for myself. Father says Dippity is not to go to the playhouse any more, because he feels that the shame of what Kit has done reflects on our family. And if Dippity does not go there, I cannot. The scrivener's shoulder is better, so I have no excuse. And without going to the playhouse, there is little chance for me to see Jeremy. Unless he looks for me? Oh, he will, I am sure of it!

Before I left for Kit's cottage, I had the clever idea of asking Miranda to go with me. Then my meeting with Rose Hamble might not be so awful.

Luckily, Miranda was indoors when I called and she clearly couldn't wait to get out. Her cheek was a little floury from baking, but I didn't bother to tell her. I also didn't tell her about Kit and the ring. She didn't ask me anything, just talked about herself.

As it turned out, the visit wasn't as bad as I'd expected. Kit was out looking for work, and the only time Rose Hamble referred to what happened was as we were leaving. She thanked me profusely for the basket of food, then pulled me back as Miranda stepped into the street.

"Patience," she said, "Kit did not take the ring."

"I am sure he didn't," I said, but I kept remembering how he stopped me reaching into his bag for the spoon.

I embraced Rose Hamble and left.

Now I am sitting in the bedroom, wondering whatever will become of me and my handsome Jeremy.

Oh dear, if I was Dippity, I would not be thinking of myself. I would be wondering what will become of Kit and his poor mother.

Aunt Sukey is calling me. What now?

LATER

When I went downstairs, I was surprised to see we had a visitor.

"Tiny!" I said. "What are you doing here?"

Aunt Sukey had kept her on the doorstep. "She wants to speak to you," she said.

"May she come in?" I asked. "She is a good girl."

Our aunt nodded, and Dippity fetched a stool for Tiny. The poor little thing still has a dreadful cough and is pale, in spite of spending all her time outdoors.

"What is it?" I asked. "Is your family well?"

"Well enough, thank you," she replied. "I been wanting to tell you something about your friend with the kind eyes."

"Kit? What about him," I asked.

"The other day, he was coming up the hill with the 'orse and cart, and a man was following him," she told me.

I was aware of Dippity and Aunt Sukey standing very still.

"Go on, Tiny," I said.

"The man reached into the cart, behind your friend's back, and opened a big bag. I think 'e might have nicked somefing. Has your friend lost anyfing?"

"I don't know," I said. "He hasn't said so. His bag is full of tools, so he might not notice until he needs something."

I glanced up at Dippity. She was frowning, as if she was concentrating very hard. Then she touched my shoulder. "Patience," she said slowly. "Maybe the man didn't take something out of Kit's bag. Maybe he put something in."

"What?" My mind whirled. "What are you saying?"

Aunt Sukey spoke then. "I know what she's saying. The ring. Maybe the man put the ring in Kit's bag."

I didn't understand.

Dippity looked confused, too. "But why would someone do that?"

"What did the man look like, girl?" said Aunt Sukey.

Tiny looked up at her. "He wore a dark green cloak with a hood pulled low, so passers-by could not see his face."

"So you would not recognize him again?" I asked.

"Oh, yes, I would," said Tiny. "I was on the ground, looking up. I saw 'is face. I would know 'im."

Dippity knelt down beside me. "Patience, we must tell someone that Kit did not steal the ring."

"We cannot know for sure."

She shook her head. "I do not believe he did." She concentrated hard. "Patience, there is a man at the playhouse who has stolen."

"Who?" I asked.

"Thomas," she said.

"A Banbury cake, Dippity!" I said. "He stole a cake!"

"And some money," she said. "I saw him, Patience. But he noticed me looking and told me not to say anything to anyone, or – or, it would be the worse for me."

Aunt Sukey took off her apron. "There is only one thing to do," she said, "and that is the right thing. We must take this child to the playhouse and let her show us who that person is. Then we can challenge him. If it is this Thomas, so be it. Come along, your father is there right now, and he will help us."

I was in turmoil. If Thomas had done this thing to Kit... Why? Was it to help Jeremy? How much did Jeremy know? If he was challenged, might he drag Jeremy into it? Oh no...

"But the man might not be from the playhouse," I said desperately. "He could have been anyone, from anywhere."

"Don't be ridiculous, Patience," said Aunt Sukey. "The ring was stolen from some room there, you know that. The thief must come from there."

I groaned inwardly. "But it will be very hard for Tiny to be sure which is the man," I said. "If she makes a mistake people will be angry with her and ... and ... and Father might get banned from the playhouse!"

But Tiny had reached out her good hand to touch mine.

"I will not make a mistake, Patience," she said. "I watch people's faces all day, to see if they are kind. I never, ever forget even one, I don't."

"That is settled," said Aunt Sukey. "If nothing is said, Kit will suffer, and your father is suffering anyway. Goodness, Patience, your father's future and the future of this family depends on us proving Kit's innocence. Do not even hesitate!"

She fetched her shawl. "Dippity and I will go to the

playhouse, and ask your father not to leave, as we will soon know who the thief is." She looked down at Tiny.

"You are quite sure you can tell us which man it is?"

Tiny nodded. "Yes, Mistress."

Aunt Sukey put a hand on Tiny's shoulder. "You are a good girl," she said. "I am sorry about your hand."

I was getting fidgety. "What shall I do?" I asked.

Aunt Sukey looked at me as if I was simple. "Fetch Kit, of course, and keep Tiny with you. Don't let her out of your sight."

So, with Tiny's little feet twinkling along beside me, I went as fast as I could to the Hambles' cottage, praying Kit would be in. I was also praying that Thomas, if he was the thief, would not involve Jeremy. I wanted to say to God, "If I can have only one prayer answered, make it that last one."

But my first prayer was answered. Kit opened the door.

"You didn't steal the ring," I said.

He turned away. "I know that."

I followed him inside, took his elbow and pulled him round to face me. "Tiny saw someone put something into your tool bag. It has to have been the ring."

I heard a gasp and saw, over his shoulder, Rose Hamble with her hand to her mouth.

Kit knelt down and spoke to Tiny, looking straight into her eyes. "Is this true?"

She nodded. "You was kind to me. I wanted to help you."

He looked at me then. I glanced down. "So do I, Kit."
I explained about Aunt Sukey going to the playhouse with
Dippity to find Father.

When I'd finished, Kit turned to his mother, bent his
head and kissed her gently, saying, "I will return soon."

I remembered that once I longed for him to kiss me.

He grabbed his hat from a hook and said, "Let us leave."

As we approached the river, we could see that carts were
blocking the entrance to the bridge. There was probably a
herd of sheep making their slow and steady way across.

Kit shouted for a wherry, and we climbed in, with him
carefully helping Tiny to a seat.

"Hurry, boatman," he said.

"That I will, sir," came the reply, as the oars dipped into
the water and began to pull us across the river. "Tide's strong
today, though."

It was indeed. I looked towards the bridge, where the
water boiled and churned through the arches. It was said to
be one of the most dangerous parts of the river, because of
the way the water had to force its way through small spaces
between the bridge supports.

We must have been more than three quarters of the way
across the busy river, when Tiny gave a sharp cry.

"There!"

She was pointing at a wherry coming in the opposite
direction, from the south bank.

When I saw who was in it, I cried out, without thinking. "Jeremy!"

But Tiny was on her knees, still pointing, shouting, "That's 'im! That's the one what did it!"

"What?" I said, in panic. "Tiny, no!"

"'Tis the one what did it," she insisted.

Jeremy's voice floated across the water. "Make for that wherry, boatman!"

As they drew near, he called, "Patience, leave that thief. Come with me!"

I shook my head. My throat was dry.

"The little carpenter's finished now," he yelled. "He won't interfere with us again."

I shook my head again, unable to speak, but Tiny pointed again and cried, "You done it! You put the thing in his bag. I saw you!"

As his boat bobbed nearer to ours, I could not believe how my handsome Jeremy's face changed. He looked down his nose as if she was a pile of dirt, and snarled at her.

"The beggar girl... Here!" He fished in his pouch, grabbed the side of our wherry with one hand and held out a handful of pennies with the other. "Here!"

"I don't understand..." said Kit.

I glanced at him. He was holding on to the side of the wherry as it rocked. He looked confused.

"Have a care, sir!" cried Jeremy's boatman. Both he and

our man were struggling with their oars, trying to hold the boats steady in the fast-running water.

Now Jeremy turned on him. "Watch your mouth, man. Here, beggar girl – take the money. Go away. Stay away!"

Tiny shrank from him, shaking her head.

Kit seemed to have gathered his wits. He leaned forward. "You!" he cried. "It was *you*! You stole the ring!" He looked from me to Jeremy and back again. "*He* put it in my bag!"

I was crying. "Yes," I sobbed.

"Patience!" Jeremy said through gritted teeth. "I did it for you!" He reached for my hand and the boat rocked dangerously.

I grabbed Kit's arm to steady myself.

"Patience," said Jeremy, "make the beggar take the money and disappear."

"No."

Then he rose up, made a grab for Tiny and, as the boat rocked, fell against her.

Next second, they were both in the water.

I screamed, holding on to Kit for dear life. Jeremy was reaching for the side of his boat, but Tiny – Tiny was floundering and drifting away.

"Jeremy, catch her!" I screamed.

But the oarsman was helping him back into his wherry. He turned, spat and said, "I'm not risking my life for a beggar."

It all happened so quickly. As Tiny was swept towards the bridge and the boiling, roiling water, Kit jumped into the river.

I saw Tiny slip beneath the surface – I saw her thin arms stretching up – I saw Kit reach for her – I saw him grab that poor little hand – I saw the pair of them swept against the side of a fisherman's boat – I saw the fisherman reaching down to grasp Tiny's little body. And I saw Kit swept away beneath the arches of London Bridge.

It seemed hours before Tiny and I were reunited on the south shore. I hugged her and she shook and cried.

"I must find Kit," I said. "Go home and get dry, Tiny."

"S'all right, Patience," she said. "I been wet afore, and it's a fine evening." She wiped her nose on her sleeve. "We'll look together."

I prayed as we ran eastwards along the bank. My eyes searched the water as I ran, trying to beat the current so poor Kit wouldn't get swept away from me. I never stopped praying, and I nearly fell to my knees in a mixture of fear and relief when in the distance, I saw a man in a little boat, pulling Kit from the water. He rowed to the bank and was just lifting him on to the muddy, empty shore when I reached him.

I thanked the man, who said, "I reckon he's gorn, Mistress," and pushed his boat back into the river. "Hit 'is head on my boat, he did," he shouted back. "Cor, it was a crack!"

Tiny caught up with me. The poor thing stood bent over, coughing, trying to catch her breath.

Between us, we managed to drag Kit clear of the water's edge, for who knew when the tide would turn and flood the shore? We pulled him up against a stack of empty fish boxes, and he lay there in the shadows as I cried.

"Turn 'im over," said Tiny. "You got to get the water out of 'im."

She helped me and as we rolled him on to his front, to my joy, he choked, then spluttered, water pouring from his mouth.

But he stayed still. I could barely feel him breathing.

"He's so cold, Patience," said Tiny. "You 'ave to keep 'im warm."

I looked around. It was growing dark and there were no lights nearby. I dare not send Tiny to knock on any doors, for who knew what might happen to her? But I needed help.

"Tiny, you have suffered enough for us," I said, "but will you do one more thing? Go and find Father, Dippity, Aunt Sukey, anybody, and bring them to me?"

"I will," she said, her thin little body shivering. "It will warm me up," she said, and she coughed again.

"Go," I said. "I will keep Kit warm."

And I did. I lay alongside him in the gloom, with my arms round him and my body pressed against his coldness.

I grew cold, too, and sleepy, but I never left him. How

could I have been so hateful to him – gentle, kind Kit, who has suffered and nearly drowned because of me and my love for Jeremy.

Love? I thought it was love. Was it love? Or something else?

Time passed as I lay shivering and waiting. I remember talking to Kit, and praying, and kissing his face a hundred times, and begging him to speak to me. I remember feeling sleepy and struggling to stay awake. I remember being so cold, and wondering how I could hope to warm Kit's body with mine. Then I remember hearing voices, and feeling hands lifting me. Gentle hands…

The next thing I knew was the warmth of my own bed, and Aunt Sukey fussing around me.

"Kit?" I asked. "Is he…?"

"He will be well, with rest and warmth and good food," she said. "His mother is here, and will stay until he is fit to leave."

I turned over and sobbed with relief, and I remember Dippity coming and kissing me and holding my hand for hours.

And then I slept. The sun was high when I woke and went downstairs.

"Where is Kit?" I asked Aunt Sukey.

"He will be down directly," she said. "He is being fed good warming stew by his mother, and I am quite sure she will not let him stir until it is gone."

When Rose Hamble came down with her tray and talked by the fire with Aunt Sukey, I slipped upstairs to where Kit lay, as if asleep.

He opened his eyes when he heard me. "Patience!" he said, and held out a hand.

I took that hand, and stroked his forehead. "Kit, I am so sorry," I began, but he hushed me.

"Do not say sorry to me," he murmured. "You saved my life. For my mother's sake, if not for my own, I can never thank you enough."

I looked at his dear face. Why had I never seen before what a good, kind young man he is? I can only think that I was blinded by Jeremy's handsome face and his wealth and breeding.

But now, when Kit was so nearly lost to us, now I know what true goodness is. He has always cared for me, maybe even loved me once, though I feel sure he no longer does. And he cares for Dippity and is nothing but sweetness and gentleness to his mother.

Yet when he held my hand and looked into my eyes, I almost thought he still cares for me and – why did I not see it before and save us all this anguish? – I know I care for him.

I love him, and it took nearly losing him to make me realize it.

"Patience!" came a shout from below. "Your father is here."

Kit squeezed my hand. "You must go," he said.

"*Patience!*"

"Coming, Aunt!" I hurried downstairs.

Father looked exhausted. He reached out for me and hugged me. "I thank the Lord that you are safe," he said.

"I must tell—" I began, but he hushed me.

"I know what happened on the river," he said. "De la Motte's boatman told all, how he tried to bribe the little beggar girl, and how de la Motte might have saved her, if he hadn't been so concerned for his own skin."

"Father, he would have let her drown, rather than be found out," I said. I was crying softly. "Was he caught?"

"Master Shakespeare has gone to find his lodgings," was the reply. "I go now to join him. De la Motte has a great deal to answer for – to me."

Aunt Sukey handed him a hunk of bread. "Eat this on the way, Harry."

"I will," he said, and was gone.

I sat on the bench. Something was nagging at me. My mind felt cloudy, as if it was full of porridge.

Suddenly, I knew what it was.

I leapt up. "Tiny!" I cried. "Where is Tiny?"

Aunt Sukey and Rose Hamble looked at each other. Then Aunt Sukey spoke.

"Patience, she is upstairs, and Dippity is tending to her. But she is not well. Not well at all."

I flew up the stairs and into the tiny back room where we keep a mattress on the floor. Dippity was sitting beside it, holding a little hand in hers, and I saw Tiny's pale sweet face on the pillow. Her eyes were closed and her breathing was jerky and hoarse.

"How is she?" I asked.

"She is very ill," said Dippity. "Aunt Sukey said her chest is bad."

I groaned. "It is all my fault. I should have sent her somewhere warm instead of letting her search for Kit with me. She was so wet and cold."

Dippity rubbed the little hand between hers. "Aunt Sukey said she was ill anyway."

But all I could remember was me telling her to run for help. "Oh, the poor little thing," I said, and I burst into tears.

"Don't cry," said Dippity. "We must be quiet and help her to get better."

I leaned against my sister. "She will not get better," I said. "Dippity, you don't understand. She will die."

Dippity smiled. "No."

"Yes, Dippity."

"No," she said again. "Aunt Sukey said she will get better if we give her warmth and good broth, and not let her sit out by the church in all weathers."

Oh, the relief! I hugged Dippity, then asked, "Are you sure? I will ask Aunt Sukey."

I flew downstairs, and what Dippity had said was confirmed.

"We do not know where she lives," said Aunt Sukey, "so as soon as she is well enough, she can take you to her home."

I was about to go up again, to sit with Kit, when Father returned, with Master Shakespeare.

"Is Kit well enough to come down?" Father asked.

"I will ask him," I said, and bounded upstairs.

In a few moments, Kit, his mother, my father, Master Shakespeare and Aunt Sukey were all sitting round the table. The news was that Jeremy had disappeared from his lodgings. He had escaped. Part of me was angry, and part of me was relieved that the beautiful man I thought I'd loved would not come to an agonizing end.

Kit said nothing.

Then Father poured a drink for Master Shakespeare and said to him, "You have more information, do you not?"

"I do." He looked at me as he spoke. "Jeremy was not who he purported to be. He was not Jeremy de la Motte at all. According to his neighbours, his real name is Jeremiah Mudd, and he seems to have lied about his background to all of us at the Globe, and to you, Patience."

I felt my face flush.

Master Shakespeare smiled grimly. "He has lied so well that we all fell for it. He will actually be a great loss to the Chamberlain's Men. He is probably one of the best players we have ever had – after all, he managed to fool the lot of us with his acting skill!"

There was a long silence. Then Aunt Sukey sent Kit back upstairs to rest.

Jeremy – Jeremiah – has gone from my life for ever. My heart aches a little for the joyous moments I had with him, but I realize now that I was never completely at ease with him. Maybe I was afraid that he would go too far, and that I would give in to temptation. I don't know.

SATURDAY SEPTEMBER 18TH

Kit is well, but is spending the day with us, resting, before returning to his home tomorrow.

And Tiny… She is still quite ill, but was well enough this afternoon to be carried downstairs by Father to sit with us all for a while. She was shy and stayed close to my sister, who was embroidering a cuff.

When we had all finished talking about the events of the last few days, Father asked Kit when he would like to start back to work.

"At once, Master," said Kit.

Everyone laughed.

"Well, tomorrow – no, 'tis Sunday tomorrow. On Monday!" he said. "I am right glad to still have my job," he added.

Father smiled and patted his shoulder. "I am glad, too, Kit. You have a fine future ahead of you."

All this while, Tiny had been admiring Dippity's sewing. When my sister stopped to flex her fingers, Tiny picked up the needle in her good hand. "I would like to do this work," she said softly.

Dippity looked thoughtful. "You would need help to thread your needles," she said. "You could surely hold the material in your bad hand and stitch with the good one. Couldn't she, Aunt Sukey?"

"I'm sure she could."

My sister smiled. "Tiny, I would like to teach you."

The little mite's eyes widened. "Would you? Would you, really? Oh, thank you. Oh, I'm so 'appy. Dippity, you're the cleverest lady I've ever met!"

Dippity looked round at everyone, eyes shining. I felt so proud that my sister could do this thing.

"Tiny," I said, "I cannot teach you like my sister can, but I will always thread your needles for you!"

We laughed, and when Kit caught my eye, looking at me with such approval, I felt warmth steal right through my body.

Father got up. "I'm going to feed Blossom," he said. "Patience, why don't you take Kit into the garden for some fresh air?"

As we walked outside, Father came between us and put an arm round our shoulders.

"You are good friends again, I hope," he said. "Aunt Sukey and I always said you should be good friends. That would fit in well with Kit's future in my business."

He stopped and pulled us round to face him. "*Are* you good friends?"

I looked into Kit's lovely brown eyes. Together, we nodded and said, "We are."

Then, as Father walked off towards the yard, whistling, Kit and I wandered in among the fruit trees. The sun was going down, and the gillyflowers were just beginning to give off their evening scent.

"Patience," Kit began.

But I needed to speak before he said how much he despised me for the way I'd behaved. "I'm sorry," I began, and then it all burst out of me. "I'm sorry I didn't believe in you; well, I did, but then you snapped at me when I went to get the spoon out of your bag so when they found the ring in there I believed you had taken it and were afraid I would see—"

He put a finger to my lips. "I wouldn't let you put your hand into my bag because there are sharp tools in it. I could not let you cut yourself."

I was filled with remorse. I had thought badly of him when he was concerned only for my safety. "Oh Kit, I'm so sorry," I said again.

"Don't be. As Master Shakespeare is forever saying when things go wrong at the playhouse, 'All's well that ends well.' I have my job back, and I am working with a master I respect. I am happy, Patience."

As I realized that his happiness was because he has his job back, and had nothing to do with caring for me, I also realized how much I love him. Without warning, my tears began to flow. "I've ruined everything," I cried. "You and Tiny nearly died because of me. How can you ever think well of me again?"

"Patience," he said softly, taking my hand and moving behind a gnarled apple tree, out of sight of everybody. "I – I care for you. I always have."

"And I for you!"

Then, as if our minds were thinking as one, we said together, "I love you."

I began to cry again, with joy. He wiped the tears from my cheeks, and I reached up to touch his face. How could I have been so blind that I didn't see how good, how kind, how gentle ... how *wonderful* Kit is.

I moved closer to him. "If you want to, you could kiss me."

His arm went round my neck, and he did not have to pull me to him. I touched my lips to his.

It was the sweetest kiss. So tender.

HISTORICAL NOTE

Play-going was a hugely popular form of entertainment in Elizabethan times. A large proportion of the population of London, as well as visitors from the country and tourists from abroad, could afford to treat themselves to an afternoon watching a play. Indeed, many people came so regularly that the companies found it necessary to change the programme daily, spending the morning rehearsing a play for the next day, before going on stage that afternoon. At the Globe, many of those plays were written by William Shakespeare. He wrote wonderful parts for women, as well as for men, but the Elizabethans would not accept women on the stage. Those parts were taken by boys and young men; beard growth and voice changes seemed to have occurred considerably later than is usual nowadays.

Shakespeare was once described as a man for all time. He could never have dreamed, as he strode on stage to act in his latest play, that other actors would be performing that same play four hundred years later. Not only would it be performed in London, but all over the world. His timeless stories have been made into movies, books, cartoons, musicals, operas and ballet and translated into many languages.

Many people consider William Shakespeare to be the greatest playwright ever. How fitting then that, thanks to the vision of a 20th-century American actor and film producer called Sam Wanamaker, Shakespeare's plays can now be enjoyed in a setting that's as close as possible to the original: the Globe Theatre on the south bank of London's River Thames.

No one knows exactly what Shakespeare's Globe playhouse looked like, but a lot of research went into making the new Globe Theatre as near to the original as possible, and Elizabethan building techniques were used in the reconstruction. To step into the Globe is to step back in time.

TIMELINE: SHAKESPEARE AND THE GLOBE

1564 William Shakespeare is born in Stratford-upon-Avon, the son of a glove-maker.

1582 William marries Anne Hathaway, a farmer's daughter, about eight years his senior.

1594 William is a member of the Chamberlain's Men, a popular company of players.

1599 The Globe opens and is an instant success.

1603 James I of England becomes king on the death of Elizabeth I; the Chamberlain's Men become known as the King's Men.

1613 The company's cannon is fired during a performance of *Henry VIII*, and sets fire to the thatched roof. A couple of hours later, the playhouse is a smouldering ruin.

1614 The Globe is rebuilt. No thatch this time; there's a tiled roof instead.

1616 William Shakespeare dies in Stratford-upon-Avon.

1642 Parliament closes all the playhouses.

1644 The Globe is pulled down, so new homes can be built on the site.

1970 Sam Wanamaker founds the Shakespeare Globe Trust,

and begins bringing his dream of recreating the Elizabethan playhouse to realization.

1997 The new Globe Theatre is opened by Her Majesty Queen Elizabeth II. It is an instant success, and is visited by people from all over the world.